I0722665

Right as Rain:
An Enemies-to-Lovers Romance
Book Two in the North Bay Series

By Stephanie Giese

Copyright © 2025 Stephanie Giese
All rights reserved

The characters and events portrayed in this book are fictitious. Any similarity to real persons, living or dead, is coincidental and not intended by the author.

No part of this book may be reproduced, or stored in a retrieval system, or transmitted in any form or by any means, electronic, mechanical, photocopying, recording, or otherwise, without express written permission of the publisher.

ISBN-13: 9781737206859

Cover design by: Rachel Howard
Interior illustrations by: Abigail Giese

Published by Binkies and Briefcases, LLC

Printed in the United States of America

Dedication:
To everyone striving for perfection and falling short,
You are good enough exactly the way you are.

Content Warning

The reader should be aware that this book contains adult content and is recommended for readers over the age of eighteen. While this is a generally light-hearted romance, the following pages also contain strong language and on-page consensual sexual encounters as well as: anxiety, alcohol, instances of emotional abuse, food insecurity, struggles with body image, mentions of addiction and treatment, post-traumatic stress, family estrangement, previous loss of a parent, medical emergencies, disordered eating patterns, and discussions about sexual harassment. This book contains detailed descriptions of mental health concerns and treatment. Human and animal deaths are also referenced but occur off the page. Jake and Alice's book is a love story with themes of trauma, loss, and grief. I promise there is a happy ending.

A Note from the Author

Thank you for visiting North Bay! The books in this series are standalone romances with interconnected characters. You do not need to read the other books in the North Bay series to be able to enjoy this one. However, there are some references that will be spoilers if the books are read out of order. In order to have the best understanding of this town and the quirky characters who live here, I recommend readers start with Book One, *Out of Left Field*.

From the beginning, my primary goal for this series has been to tell fun and engaging stories that show realistic examples of consent and emotional support. My books have a strong focus on mental health and treatment. Jake and Alice are very special to me. They were the first characters from North Bay who appeared to me, and they are both struggling to come to terms with some tough stuff. Unlike other books in the North Bay series, this is not a sports romance. I classify this book as a friendly enemies-to-lovers story.

As always, there is plenty of humor and heart, but there are also multiple difficult and sensitive topics addressed in these pages, so I highly encourage you to check out the content warnings. This story was difficult to write. Jake and Alice have been through a lot, both together and separately. These two fought me throughout the entire process almost as much as they fought each other. I'm so excited to finally be able to share their journey with you!

Chapter 1

Alice

The cars whip past, and I grip the steering wheel for dear life as I take the final curve, focused on passing the red blur to my right while I chase my friends in circles around an indoor track. I groan as Jacob Gibson maneuvers his car away from mine and pulls ahead toward the finish line. When the countdown clock on the wall winds down, the go-karts roll to a stop, and I wrestle myself out of my harness.

Jordan and Shelley are still behind me, which means I took second place out of the four of us. There are plenty of other people who had better times than I did, but those strangers aren't the ones making me twitchy about this loss. Normally, I wouldn't care, but of course I had to lose to *him*. I sit and glare at Jake. When he notices me staring, he laughs and waves, so I huff and look away. I don't know why I never seem to get under his skin as much as he gets under mine.

I'm still seated when Shelley walks up to my car and speaks to me in a low voice. "Will you hate me if I drive home with Jordan? I know you and Jake aren't exactly besties. I'm not trying to break girl code, but..." She bites her bottom lip, and her voice trails off while her eyes drift to where Jordan is standing a few cars down. When Jake jogs right past us to talk to him, Shelley turns back to me. "I won't leave you by yourself with Jake if he really makes you uncomfortable."

I laugh. "Uncomfortable is one word for it. Other words might be distressed, disturbed, annoyed. You get the idea. He's not my favorite, but Jake's harmless. I've been dealing with him for literally my entire life. I'll be fine."

On the way here, she and I drove together, and the guys were in a separate car. Shelley's our friend Mike's younger sister, and she's only in town for a short visit. But she needed a night out because her brother is off tonight hooking up with my best friend, who also happens to be Jake's best friend. Honestly, it's about time. Mike and our BFF, Danielle, have been playing an exhausting game of *will they or won't they* for a while. They finally made it official at karaoke earlier tonight and went back to his place to celebrate. The rest of us are trying to stay out of their way for a few hours. Driving out of town to occupy Jake, Shelley, and Jordan with some go-karting seemed like such a good idea two hours ago.

I appreciate Shelley for trying to look out for me, but it's obvious she's crushing hard on her brother's roommate, and who am I to deny her a shot at some alone time with Jordan? Even if it means, by default, I'll be stuck making the forty-minute drive home with the most annoying know-it-all playboy on the planet.

I take off my helmet and try to shake out my hair. I'm sure the spikey intentional bedhead look I worked hard to perfect is completely flattened. "Just know you'll probably be called to testify at my trial if I strangle him. Or better yet, you can be my lawyer. You're going to law school next year, right?"

I thought I could handle one night with Jake for my best friend's sake because at least we'd have other people with us. I can't promise not to throttle him if we're left alone.

"Thanks. Danielle was right. You really are the best." Shelley smiles.

"Remember this, because I fully plan to cash in on a return favor someday."

"Deal." She waves a quick goodbye before running off to meet up with Jordan. He turns to give me a nod, then shakes Jake's hand before he and Shelley head out.

There are only fifteen minutes before this place closes for the night, and they're already shutting off the lights in the arcade area. Time to get on with the unbearable part of the evening. As I step out of my car, a little boy exits his own go-kart and runs toward his parents.

"Mom, mom, mom, did you see me? Can we get ice cream now?" He's barreling ahead at full speed, and with the go-kart blocking the other side, I have nowhere to go when he crashes into me.

"Oof." I fall back into my car, scraping my hip on the steering wheel and twisting my ankle on the way down. None of it is as painful as the sharp sting of embarrassment I feel from everyone's stares.

The boy looks up at me and glares. "Watch where you're going, lady. Mo-om. This lady was in the way, and I fell down." He's pointing at me, even though we are only inches apart.

"I see that. I'm so sorry, baby. Grown-ups should pay closer attention. Let's get you some ice cream." His mother comes through the gate to scoop him up, and she carries him away. She shoots me a dirty look in the process, like I wasn't minding my own business when her little cherub knocked into me.

I roll my eyes and try to ignore the extra attention from everyone who saw me fall. I'm sure my face is as pink as my hair as I attempt to pull myself out of the car again. It's a struggle this time, with my butt firmly wedged between the seat and the steering wheel.

Jake appears and yanks me out by the arm.

"You good, Louse?"

"I think so."

Yep. Jake calls me Louse, as in the singular form of head lice, because in the seventh grade he found it hilarious that Alice spells "a lice." Ten years later, not much has changed.

"Although, as always, I would be even better if you weren't touching me," I say as he stands me up. I cringe as my right foot touches down, and I fight the impulse to lean on him.

"Then maybe try learning to avoid collisions with small children."

"Shut up. It was his fault. And I'm fine."

But when I try to walk, pain shoots through my ankle and I wince. Ugh. I do not need to deal with this right now. Not in front of Jake. Jerk kid. This is exactly why I'm never having any little crotch goblins of my own. I suck in a deep breath and try to walk again.

"*Ouch.*" This time a small yelp escapes on its own.

"Okay, tough guy. Sit back down. I'll get some ice," Jake tells me. But I don't want to take orders from him, and I hate how there are still so many eyes on me as the next round of wannabe drivers are impatiently waiting for their turn.

"First of all, I'm a tough *girl.* No, not girl. Woman. And can you just—" I'm not actually sure what I want him to do, so I let the sentence hang. I don't mean to sound so angry, but I'm embarrassed and in pain, and I hate having all this attention on me.

Jake laughs at my protest, causing even more people to look our way. He rolls his eyes and picks me up so I'm lying across both of his annoyingly strong, tattooed arms. Instinctively, I start to wrap my arms around his neck, but then I think better of it and cross them over my chest instead. He chuckles again.

"Glad you're finding this amusing," I snap.

He doesn't respond, just sets me down in a chair by the snack bar and asks the teenagers working for a cup of ice. He puts a lid on it and wraps it in a handful of napkins from the dispenser before handing it to me.

"Here. Give me your keys. I'm driving your car home."

God, he's so bossy. I can't stand that looking up at him from this angle makes me notice the way his anime t-shirt stretches across his pecs.

"You wish I'd let you touch Bertie." It took me years to save up for my lime green vintage Volkswagen Beetle, and I'm very protective of her.

"Guess we're spending the night here then, because you couldn't even walk the twenty feet from the track to the snack bar just now. You really think you're going to be able to drive on that foot?"

It's so irritating when he has a point. His dark hair falls into his face, and as he brushes it away, it's hard not to notice the veins popping on his arms. I would rather die than let anyone catch me ogling Jacob Gibson. He would never let me hear the end of it. But it's not my fault he's filled out so much this year and finally grown into his formerly lanky body. He has always been tall, but then again almost everyone is taller than me. This year he's gotten broader. He must be spending a lot more time in the gym.

I want to argue, but I truly can't put any weight on my foot, so I don't know how I would be able to use the pedals. Reluctantly, I let him scoop me up again and carry me to the passenger's seat of my own car. I try to put my foot on the dashboard and lean the cup against it, but the ice won't stay put, so I root through my purse, trying to find a headband or something else I might be able to use to secure it to my ankle. Unfortunately, it only contains my wallet, my phone, and an old bag from the craft store. I don't think the stickers, gel pens, and glitter from last week's trip with Danielle will be much help.

I have a fleeting thought to sprinkle the glitter over Jake's head, but when I realize I would be the one left to clean it off Bertie's seats, I give up. I move my foot back to the floor, where I wedge the cup of ice between my ankle and the wall.

Jake's brow creases. "Do you want to go over to the Urgent Care and get an X-ray while we're in Marnock?" he asks as we pull out of the crowded parking lot. We drove for forty minutes to get here tonight, which means we're closer to health care. North Bay, our hometown, is too small to have its own 24-hour access to a medical center. "We're almost there already."

"No, I think I just rolled it. It will probably be better in a day or two." I don't know if that's true, but either way, I can't afford to be taking on any medical bills for small things like this. If they send me to the Emergency Room for more tests or a cast, it could add up to thousands of dollars I don't have. "Um, thanks for the ice." I look straight ahead, not wanting to make eye contact. "Do you think you can just take me to Honey's house? That way we don't have to worry about getting you back to your car." Honey Daniels is Danielle's grandmother and Jake's neighbor.

"Nah, I can take you home. I'll just have someone come pick me up from your place."

"No," I insist. "I'd rather go to Honey's. Just drive."

It's no secret that my house is not a fun place to be. Everybody in North Bay knows Earl Caulfield is a hot mess. Tonight will be no different, especially if my dad sees I hurt myself and he might need to help me pay for a doctor. Danielle lives with her grandma, and Honey lets me stay with them as often as I like, which is much more often lately as Dad's mood seems to hover at some constant level of grump. Thankfully, Jake doesn't argue.

"Fine. Ms. Honey's it is."

Jake's the only one of us who has ever called Honey Daniels *Ms.* Honey. I don't even think Honey likes it, but Jake's mom is obsessed with propriety, and she said if their neighbor was going to allow her son to address her by her first name, then the least he could do was respect her title. She drilled it into him so much when we were kids that he still does it. I smirk remembering the way Mrs. Gibson used to pinch Jake's arm every time he forgot.

He clears his throat, and I think I see his grip on the steering wheel tighten a bit before he reaches over to fool with the radio. I swat his hand away from my dashboard. "Don't touch Bertie."

"How exactly do you suggest I drive your car without touching it?"

I have no retort for that, so I fold my arms over my chest and stew as he continues down the darkened street. Before we leave

Marnock, he pulls into the gas station. "I'm going to grab a soda. You want one?" he asks in an uncharacteristic show of thoughtfulness.

"No. I'm fine." I lean down to readjust the dripping cup against my skin, which is now numb from the ice. As I straighten up again, I catch myself staring at Jake's wide shoulders as he walks inside. When did he get so freaking hot? It's really unfair. He was our valedictorian in high school, and he just finished his third year riding an academic toward his college degree. People who come from rich families shouldn't be allowed to also be smart and good-looking. Especially when they have obnoxious personalities.

When Jake comes back, he opens the driver's side door and puts two Cokes in the cupholders between us, then he turns around and starts pumping gas into my car.

"What are you doing? I said I don't want one. I have a job. I can buy my own Coke. And I can pump my own gas," I yell through the open door. I might be tight on cash sometimes, but I can pay my own way. I don't need a rich boy to buy me drinks or gasoline. I take care of myself.

Jake bends to stick his head through the doorframe.

"Relax, Lousy. You drove out here. I'll cover the gas to get us home. This is how normal people function." He speaks in an exaggerated calm tone as if to highlight how crazy he thinks I am. "I realize that might be a new concept for you."

"Whatever. Just take me to Honey's." I twist the cap off my soda bottle and attempt to take a sip, but it bubbles over and erupts, splattering all over me.

"*Ugh!*" I screech. "Did you do this on purpose?"

The two of us have a low-key prank war going on with each other. We do that kind of thing all the time, but tonight I am not in the mood.

Jake laughs diabolically as he gets back in the car and twists the cap off his own drink. His hardly fizzes at all, and he takes a long drag from the bottle before looking at me.

"Nope. I can't say shaking yours up a little didn't cross my mind, but I didn't do it. Although it was hilarious. This time it was pure karma. The universe agrees with me, you need to lighten up a little."

"Easy for you to say when you aren't the one whose lap is completely soaked."

His expression changes, and for a millisecond I could swear there is a flash of heat in his eyes, but it disappears just as quickly. I bend to unwrap the wilted napkins from my cup of ice and use them to try to mop up my clothes.

Jake produces a small pack of peanuts and uses his teeth to tear them open. He pours half the package into his soda and holds out the rest to me, but I ignore the offer. I turn away from him and look out the window for the rest of the ride.

Unfortunately, when we get back to Honey's, she isn't home and her phone goes straight to voicemail. Who knows where Honey disappeared to after we saw her at karaoke earlier?

"Do you think she's still living it up at Brew-Ha-Ha?"

He shrugs. "She could be anywhere by now. Ms. Honey has always been a wild card."

There is only one other person with a key to this house, and Jake and I both know there is no way we are interrupting Danielle to get her to let us in.

"Come on." Jake motions to his parents' huge waterfront house, which is directly across the street from Honey's much more modest rancher. He and Danielle grew up neighbors, whereas my family was on the other side of town. They rode the bus together every day, but I lived close enough to ride my bike to school.

"What? No. I'm not going home with you." Although, I don't want to go back to my house either. I just can't deal with that right now.

"I'm not seeing a lot of options here, Louse."

I glance around. One night in Bertie wouldn't be the worst thing.

"No. Absolutely not. No way am I agreeing to let you sleep in your car right in front of my perfectly decent house." Jake huffs. Add to his obnoxious personality the fact that he seems to be able to read my mind.

"Well, good thing you have no say in how I spend my nights. I'll be fine. Honey will come home eventually."

The largest waterfront property in North Bay is a lot more than "perfectly decent." It's intimidating, and it's a reminder of how different our lives really are. It wouldn't be the first time I've slept in my car to avoid my dad, but I don't think anyone knows that.

North Bay is a safe neighborhood. Honestly, I'm surprised Honey even locks her doors. I wish she hadn't, because then we could have avoided this whole predicament. Besides, my ankle is already starting to feel better. Kind of. Maybe. Okay, fine. It still hurts a lot.

Jake takes a deep breath as he rolls his head in a slow circle. It appears his patience with me is wearing thin. Well, bro, same.

"Don't fight me on this, Lousy. It's getting late, your clothes are wet, and this has been a stupidly long day. We're going over to my place. It's right there. My parents aren't home. They're at some marriage retreat near the beach. I'll take their room and you can sleep in mine. Besides, I still have your keys. So, actually, I do have a say in this."

He holds the keys over my head and laughs while I try to reach up and grab them. I'm in no state to jump, but even if I could, Jake is a full foot taller than I am, so it's pointless trying to fight him.

There might have been a time before everything that happened in high school when sleeping in Jacob Gibson's bed would have seemed like a dream come true. Now it's just an inconvenience I don't seem to be able to avoid tonight. It probably would be a good idea to elevate my foot, and that's hard to do in the car. Plus, these damp, sticky clothes really are uncomfortable.

"Come on," he says, pocketing my keys again. "You can see Hazel."

With that, he knows he's won. As annoying as I find her owner, I love that sweet fifteen-year-old bulldog. It will be worth putting up with Jake tonight if I can convince Hazel to sleep snuggled up with me.

"Fine." I blow out a breath. I realize he's being pretty helpful tonight and I sound like an ungrateful brat, so I try to rein it in. I refuse to let him have the upper hand when it comes to matters of civility. "Thank you."

"Aw, that must have been really hard for you. Was it? Tell me how much it's killing you to admit you need me right now." He has the easy laugh of someone who doesn't know what it means to struggle.

"I hate you."

"Keep telling yourself that."

I want to wipe that smirk off his face, but instead I hobble behind him and cross the street.

Jake lets me into his bedroom and gives me privacy to clean myself up while he moves my car into the garage. The last thing we need is for his parents to find out I was here. I know I could just leave Bertie parked at Honey's so the neighbors won't gossip about seeing me parked outside the Gibsons' house overnight, but I also don't want Honey to worry when she finally gets home and sees my car, but I'm not there.

Hazel watches me with a tilted head until I finally manage to wiggle my jeans over my swollen ankle and peel off my wet shirt. Then I steal a clean tee from Jake's dresser and shove my soiled clothes from tonight into the plastic bag I found in a crumpled ball at the bottom of my purse. I take out the pens and vials of glitter to make room for my wet jeans. The glitter in my hand gives me an idea. I sprinkle a generous helping of sparkles into Jake's top drawer before making my way onto his bed.

"Don't tell him, okay?" I whisper to Hazel. "This is just between us girls." There's a set of carpeted stairs next to the bed to help her climb up with her aging, arthritic legs. "Come on, up you go," I call her to me.

I always wanted a pet, but with my mom's allergies and our limited finances, it wasn't in the cards for me. I remember being so jealous when the Gibsons brought a puppy home. Jake even got to bring Hazel for show-and-tell once in the fourth grade.

Hazel lets me bury my face into her fur and give her belly scratches, then she stretches herself out across the blanket, keeping me company while I prop my sore foot up with one of Jake's pillows. I chuckle, imagining it smelling like my sweaty feet the next time he lays down. His bed feels like a cloud, and it doesn't take long for me to drift off to sleep under his fancy down comforter. I don't wake up until I hear muffled voices.

No.

He's talking to Danielle, and it's already morning. My stomach turns. She cannot find me here. Not like this. I know she's dating Mike now, but not that long ago, before she was mesmerized by the baseball player, Danielle was all about Jake. After all the time she spent confiding in me about her major crush on the owner of this bed, it would definitely hurt her to discover me in it, sans pants, wearing nothing but his shirt, first thing in the morning.

Thankfully, she doesn't stay long. Although, I could swear I just heard Jake tell Danielle he's failed out of school. I must have misheard because that can't possibly be true. He's the smartest person I know. It's one of his most annoying qualities. He hardly had to put in any effort, and he still made straight A's in high school and went off to college on a full ride he didn't even need because his parents are loaded. Meanwhile, some of us had to spend a year renting kayaks and paddle boats to tourists before we could save up enough to enroll at the community college.

When I hear the front door close, I try to sneak into the hallway bathroom. Unfortunately, I'm slower than normal because, while it's starting to feel better and thankfully there's no bruising, my ankle is still sore. Jake sees me and calls out from the kitchen.

"Jesus, Louse. Put on some pants. Oh, and you're welcome to wear my shirt, by the way."

I flip him off and limp into the bathroom, where I slam the door and take my sweet time getting ready. I splash cold water onto my face to scrub away last night's makeup and try to finger-comb my pixie cut into behaving, then I steal a little bit of his toothpaste and brush my teeth with my finger. I may or may not also use his deodorant. What's a girl supposed to do when the alternative is walking around smelling like stale arcade aftermath? If I were at my own house, I could use a ribbon or some safety pins to make this oversized tent look like a T-shirt dress, but right now I'm swimming in it. I'm just going to have to make it work. After using the bathroom, I try to put on an air of confidence as I step back out into the hall.

"Don't even pretend you aren't fantasizing about what is happening under this shirt. And what's this I hear about you failing out of school, rich boy?" I ask, strutting to meet him in the kitchen. It may be more of a hobble than a strut, but I'm pulling it off. Mostly.

As soon as I turn the corner, I stop in my tracks.

Oh, God. Please don't let this be happening.

Jake is standing between his parents. His eyes are closed and his head is tilted up toward the ceiling, like he's trying to levitate and float out of here.

This is not good.

Mr. and Mrs. Gibson are the most buttoned-up people I've ever met, and I'm in their house first thing in the morning, completely naked under their son's faded old shirt. They definitely think something happened last night. The judgment and condemnation are written all over their faces. We are both adults, but I feel like I'm sixteen again. The Gibsons are not the kind of parents who are going to be cool with Jake having a girl spend the night in their house. Any girl. But especially me.

"Alice." The cool, detached way Ward Gibson says my name makes me feel like I've been sent to the principal's office, and my mouth is suddenly dry. "We have some family matters to discuss this morning, and Jacob will be occupied for the remainder of the day. I'm sure you can see yourself out."

Shelia doesn't say a word, but her lips are pursed, and her blonde bob stays firmly sprayed in place as she scans my body, shaking her head. I want to shrink under her stare, even though I know Jake and I didn't do anything wrong. Even if we had hooked up last night (which, *gag*), we are grown-ups capable of making our own decisions. But this is their house. They have every right to kick me out of it if I'm not welcome, and I'm obviously not.

"Oh, um, sure. I was just leaving." I use my thumb to point over my shoulder. Things immediately get even more awkward because I have to duck into Jake's bedroom to gather my stuff in order to get out of here. I grab my bags and my keys as fast as I can. Walking out of his room with a bag of last night's clothes only adds fuel to the unspoken accusation that we slept together. They all stand silently and watch from the kitchen while I fumble my way out of their house.

Jake drags a hand down his face and tries to apologize with his eyes. He can save his silent pleading. I'll never forgive him for this. Sleeping in the car would've been much more preferable. I slide my shoes on as quickly as humanly possible and throw my purse over my shoulder before I speed-limp down the hall. My ankle is still pretty sore, but it's much better than last night and I can put weight on it, so I should be able to drive home.

On my way to the garage, I can hear clearly when Jake's dad asks him, "Just what do you think you are doing using my house like this?"

Then his mom chimes in with, "Seriously, Jacob? Alice Caulfield? Have a bit more respect for yourself."

"Mom, it's not like that," Jake argues.

"I know exactly what it's like, Jacob. Don't forget your father and I were young once. You have enough problems at the moment. You don't need to add the issues someone like the Caulfield girl will bring into your life. I expect better from you."

Jake groans, but he knows even better than I do that it's pointless to fight with his mother. Still, it takes me by surprise how much it stings when I hear him say, "Yes, ma'am."

My hand is shaking when I start the engine on Bertie. My stomach clenches around the anxiety and humiliation fighting for space in my intestines, but at least I manage to back out of the driveway before any of them can see the tears.

Chapter 2

Jake

It's one thing when Alice and I rag on each other over small stuff, but it's different when someone else is getting on her case about things she can't control. What does that even mean, *someone like the Caulfield girl?*

"What do you have to say for yourself?" my dad asks.

I fight the urge to roll my eyes, attempting to have a mature conversation with him. "Come on. It was just Alice. She hurt her ankle last night and wasn't up for going home. We tried Ms. Honey's place first, but no one was there, so I brought her here. We stayed in separate rooms."

My mom finds her voice, then she clicks her tongue. "She was walking around this house half-naked only moments ago, Jacob. Wearing your shirt. Her clothes were in your room. You'll have to forgive our skepticism. In the future, I ask that you keep your conquests out of this home." Disapproval radiates off of her, which is nothing new.

No matter what I do, according to these two, it's always going to be the wrong thing. They think I'm incapable of making good decisions. The fact that I dropped out of college recently isn't helping my case, but it was the same even when I was the captain of the basketball team or graduating at the top of my class. The good stuff was expected, never celebrated. The bad stuff, however, they are more than happy to point out. Some parents might be happy their son tried to help an injured friend, but not mine. Correction and criticism are their MO. I should be used to it by now.

"Consider your future, son. A girl like that will take advantage of your generosity. It might seem fun now, but one bad decision can mean you're trapped." That's quite possibly the dumbest thing I've ever heard come out of my dad's mouth. My parents don't know her like that.

Alice would chew off her own arm before she'd willingly attach herself to me. The woman hates me. I can't pinpoint exactly when her animosity started, but I think it was toward the end of high school. We actually used to be tight, but not anymore. She didn't even want me to buy her a damn soda. The idea that she's trying to recruit me to be her sugar daddy is preposterous. I have to physically bite my tongue to keep myself from laughing in his face, and I can already taste a tinge of copper. I need to tread this line carefully though, because at least for now, I still live in their house.

"She doesn't need a meal ticket. She has a job and a home." I almost add *it's just not one she wanted to go back to last night*, but I catch myself. My parents don't need more ammunition. I don't even know why I bother to protest, it's not like Lousy and I will be sleeping in the same space ever again.

He scoffs. "That dilapidated eyesore with the overgrown weeds is not even her house. It's her father's. Women like her are always leeching off one man or another. Ask Earl, he'll tell you himself. He never intended to become a father at that age."

My fist clenches involuntarily, and I bite harder. It's insane to imply a man had no responsibility in the creation of his own child. Plus, if they think Alice is a leech for still living with her dad, what do they think of me for coming back here?

"Our son and Earl Caulfield's daughter." Mom clicks again and shakes her head.

"Mom, Dad, come on. Mrs. Caulfield is dead. And the man is a war veteran."

Alice's parents were young when they had her. Nineteen, I think. Her dad was deployed when we were little. He hasn't been the same since he got back from his second tour. When they lost her mom a few years ago, things started getting even worse. I understand why Alice tries to avoid spending too much time with her dad. He's not in a good place right now, and he takes it out on her the most.

"You forget your father and I have known that man for forty years, Jacob. He's always been quite...unkempt. Even before his misfortunes befell him." My mom's weak attempt at empathy falls short. Everyone knows she thinks the Caulfields are beneath us.

They may have all grown up together here in town, but my parents don't really know Mr. Caulfield. They definitely don't understand his daughter. Not that I get her either. Lousy has always been an enigma. My parents, on the other hand, are much less of a mystery. They're just snobs.

"Forget the girl," Dad says. "If you have time to be entertaining friends in our home, you have time for a job."

"We're concerned about you, Jacob." Mom tries to soften her tone, but her words are still clipped. She clicks her tongue again. "No schooling, no degree, no career plan, and now you're sneaking women into our home. This isn't like you. At the very least, you could ask your uncle for more responsibility and make better use of all this idle time."

"Okay, you're right," I say, more to end the conversation than anything else. Mom hums and bobs her head, pacified for now. They're wrong about a lot of that stuff, but I do need a job. "I'll call Uncle Tim and see if he has more work available." I've done a few odd jobs at his vacation rentals.

"My brother has always said there's a property management position waiting for you if you want it," Dad chimes in.

"It's a start, I suppose," Mom concedes. "But you still need to find some direction, Jacob. Do something purposeful. You don't want to be working as a handyman for the rest of your life."

There's nothing wrong with honest work, but I'm already so over this argument. I close my eyes and force myself to nod. "Sure. I'll work on finding something purposeful."

It would probably take years of therapy before I figure out what that actually means for me. But Gibsons aren't allowed to need counseling. That's for other people. People who really need it. Like the Caulfields.

"That's all we ask." My mom busies herself unpacking the large straw tote bag she took to the retreat. As she sets her sunglasses on the ceramic tray she keeps on the counter, my dad digs into his pocket and does the same with his wallet and keys. It's their way of signaling this conversation is finally over.

I blow out a frustrated breath. Hungry, but too annoyed to make breakfast, I grab a protein bar from the cabinet before heading down the hall to shut myself in my room. I flop on my bed and open the wrapper. Taking a bite, I stare up at the spinning fan while I chew.

My parents' method of delivery sucks, but they aren't totally wrong. I do need to figure out what the hell I'm doing with my life. It's starting to feel like the walls are closing in here in my childhood home, but this town has a hold on me. As aggravating as living under my parents' roof can be, North Bay gives me a sense of peace I don't have when I'm away. Being around the water, having my dog with me, and the slower pace of life in a small town help clear out the static in my brain. The one thing I don't regret about blowing up my life plan is that I'm finally back for good. Maybe I'm destined to be a townie after all. Would that be such a bad thing?

Hazel lumbers to my side. "I know, girl. You've been so patient this morning." I lean to scratch her behind the ear, and I catch a whiff of citrus on my sheets. Alice.

The sight of her in nothing but my shirt was unexpected. Maybe it's a good thing my parents came home when they did. The image of her bare legs has me riled up in a way I can't act on if I want to keep my sanity. I can't let my mind go there. Things with Alice are strained enough without making her the star of some of my more depraved fantasies.

I need to sweat it out.

"Come on, Hazel. I'll give you your breakfast and take you for a run."

It will be more like a brisk jog if we're lucky. She was a sweet, lazy brick even when she was younger, but now the poor girl definitely can't keep up with me. Still, I need the exercise. And to get out of this house.

I walk over to my dresser to grab a pair of socks, but when I open the drawer I'm greeted with a silver sparkling mess.

How does this happen? Does Alice carry a vial of glitter in her purse just in case the opportunity to annoy the hell out of people arises? She's diabolical. But I have to admit she got me good with this one. And I was even starting to feel bad about the shitty way my parents treated her. Not anymore. This was the reminder I needed. Alice Caulfield fully deserves the open can of tuna I left under the front seat of her car.

My phone buzzes in my pocket.

Louse: Why does Bertie smell like ass?

Me: ::*shrugging emoji*::

Louse: *I know you did this.*

Me: *Prove it.*

I can picture her nostrils flaring, and I chuckle. But now her face is in my head again. I shake the glitter from my socks and grab Hazel's leash. I really need to burn off some of this energy.

Present Day

Chapter 3

Alice

Chairs creak and books slam closed as everyone around me packs up their belongings and clears their desks. I can't bring myself to look away from the paper in my hand and the unnecessarily large letter C staring back at me. The grade I know for a fact I don't deserve. My face heats, and a knot forms in my stomach. I force myself to close my eyes and take a few deep breaths. When I open them again, I want to scream at the professor who is gathering his own materials.

When I signed up for Creative Writing at North Bay Community College, I thought it would be my favorite class, but lately I dread coming here each week. There are only about a dozen people taking the course, so it's impossible to hide. I also didn't realize how subjective the grading was going to be. I'm already in the process of building my career as a brand-new author. I have published some work online and I'm building an audience, albeit a small one, who seem to like my stories. I might not have tons of sales, but my books *are* selling, and they have decent reviews.

I'm here to improve my work and level-up in my career, but that's next to impossible when you're a romance writer and your aging male professor refuses to acknowledge the genre as an acceptable form of literature. I'd like to tell him to take it up with Jane Austen, but I know arguing won't do anything to change the grade on my paper. There are no notes, only the big red letter circled on the top of the first page.

When everyone else has cleared the room, I gather my things. There's a lump in my throat as I approach Professor Ratnick.

"Excuse me, sir. I'd like to ask you about my grade on this assignment."

"Ah, Mrs. Caulfield. There isn't much to discuss, I'm afraid. Mediocre work will receive mediocre grades."

I pull my lips tight and make myself count to five in my head before I speak again.

He doesn't bother to look at me while he gathers the papers from his lectern and shoves them haphazardly into his briefcase. Then he grabs his cardigan from the back of his chair.

"May I ask what about my work you consider mediocre, and what improvements you might recommend?" My hands are shaking, but I manage to keep my voice steady.

He reaches under his glasses and pinches the bridge of his nose. When he realizes I'm not leaving without an answer, he offers, "You might start with attempting the third person. Frankly, first person point of view is juvenile and unprofessional. Changing to the past tense might help. Not to mention the ending being unrealistic. You might also consider changing the gender of your protagonist. The whole thing reads like an old woman's diary."

Exactly.

"Yes, that was my intention with this piece. I wanted to explore the often-overlooked older female perspective. That's why I wrote it from the grandmother's point of view."

He ignores my point and continues with his own. "The sex scene was also gratuitous and underwhelming. No one wants to read graphic content about a character at that age."

"I see. I'll keep that in mind."

He wants me to change my point of view, rewrite the whole thing, and make it sound like it was written by a man? Yeah, that's not happening. There is also nothing gratuitous about that love scene. It moves the entire plot of my character-driven love story, unlike the scene in the short story he praised last week from Aiden, in which a male character banged a random flight attendant in the airplane bathroom for no relevant reason as he was on his way to Paris to stop a terrorist attack. There were also at least ten spelling and grammar mistakes in his three-page story. Apparently, that one was deserving of an A. I only know this because Ratnick made a huge show of using Aiden's piece as a shining example of what he expected from his students.

After this conversation, I don't care if he fails me the next time. I will be writing every other assignment in the first person, present tense with female main characters purely out of spite.

"Thank you for your time," I say, not feeling a single ounce of gratitude.

By the time I turn around, I'm already second-guessing myself.

Maybe he's right. Maybe my voice isn't ringing true because writers have to draw from their own experiences, and being loved the way my character is in this story isn't something I know. Not to mention, I'm not even close to being a grandmother.

Screw this.

I shove my way through the classroom door, out of the building, and toward the grassy area where Danielle is waiting for me so we can carpool home in her book van.

I crumple my essay and slam it down into the nearest trash can.

She looks up from her book. "Rough class, I take it?"

I groan. "I can't believe I'm paying good money to sit through this patriarchal bullshit." I march toward her van, and she falls into step beside me.

"Uh-oh. What happened?"

I give Danielle the run-down of my latest encounter with Professor There's-No-Such-Thing-As-A-Good-Female-Perspective.

"He did not." She stops short, her dark ponytail swinging as she shakes her head. "That's terrible. Are you going to report him?"

"For what? Not liking my story? It's not against any rules for him to not like my work. If I complain, it will only look like I'm whining because I can't handle criticism."

"This is so frustrating. That jerk."

"Yeah, well. What else is new? This is the kind of stupid thing women in the arts have been fighting against since the beginning of time."

"We could always sic Honey on him."

The thought makes me smile. "Ha. She could definitely take him down a peg or three. But I don't need your grandma fighting my battles for me, no matter how much fun it would be to watch Ratface crumble under the force that is Honey Daniels."

"We'll keep her on stand-by."

Knowing Danielle and Honey are in my corner does make me feel a little better.

I'm quiet on the ride home, preoccupied with thoughts about the next assignment for Ratnick. I already have a piece in mind that I think might work well, but I need to make quite a few tweaks so it fits the criteria, and I'm sure it will still only earn me another C. At this point, I'm not even sure why I'm still trying to make this writing dream work. Maybe I should just give up and try to find a full-time gig here in town. Edna would probably let me take over Danielle's old shifts at The Blue Crab.

As I'm stewing, I get a text from the zoo. It's a close-up picture of a small, furry rodent peeking its head out of a hole in the ground while it seems to look knowingly at the camera. My weekly prairie dog update never fails to make me smile, no matter how down I feel. The adorable animal pics always seem to come when I need them the most.

"At least you have book club tonight?" Danielle offers as we pull up to my house. "No grades required for that."

"Good point. Thanks for the ride." I hop out of the van and wave goodbye.

It's meeting night for Spread Those Pages, but Danielle still can't be convinced to join us. Not that I blame her. I can see how it would be weird to join an erotic book club founded by your grandma.

"Hey, Dad, I'm back," I call out as I open the door. I immediately stub my toe on what I think is a carburetor. I swear under my breath and move into the kitchen to microwave the food I meal prepped, then I deliver it to him in his recliner in the living room.

He doesn't acknowledge me or take his eyes off the TV when I set it on the tray next to him. There are days like this when my dad doesn't say a word and days he spends enraged and yelling at the world and everyone in it simply for existing. Somehow, the quiet days are the worst ones.

"Did you take your shower yet?" I ask. The faded pink stains on his white tank top make me think it's the same one he spilled tomato sauce on yesterday. He grunts and motions for me to step to the side so I'm not blocking his view.

Sighing, I spread a blanket over his lap and I pat his shoulder while I take in the rest of the room. I should really run the vacuum when I get home tonight, but I don't know how to move all Dad's junk out of the way if he's not in the right frame of mind to help.

He's always collected used car parts, but in the years since we lost my mom, the collection has gotten out of hand and slowly taken over the house. The big hunks of metal weigh too much for me to move on my own. I tell myself I'll take care of it later, then try to push down the nagging realization that Dad always says the same thing about this mess, and it hasn't been true yet.

"I need to head out again," I pause, waiting for him to answer. He doesn't. "But this time I won't be as long."

He shoos me again, grumbling a wrong answer at the game show he's watching.

I grab my dog-eared copy of the book and the dish of strawberries and chocolate hummus I put in the fridge this morning. I pull the door closed as I leave. In the yard, I cross my fingers, saying a small prayer that Bertie will start before I turn the key in the ignition. I love the old girl, but she's been giving me more than a few fits lately.

Thankfully, she cooperates, and I manage to make it over to Fringe only a few minutes after six o'clock. Book club never starts on time anyway. Honey's Honda pulls up next to me in the parking lot because she's also fashionably late.

"What did you bring?"

"Strawberries from Mom's garden and chocolate hummus."

"Oh, don't mind if I do." Honey lifts the foil on my plate to swipe a berry, then she dries her hand on the front of her hot pink tunic, not seeming to care at all when strawberry juice drips on the fabric. "I haven't been over to the garden yet this season, I didn't realize you were doing strawberries."

My mom loved to garden. When she passed away, Honey helped us start a community garden at the library in her honor. I try to get over there as often as I can.

"Brownies," she says, flashing her own container as we walk into the yoga studio/beauty parlor where we've been holding our bi-monthly meetings since we got kicked out of the library. Apparently, someone complained that the content of our literature wasn't appropriate for a taxpayer-supported space.

We cross through the empty hair studio and up the steps to the open yoga and dance space where the other ladies are already gathered.

"Hi, everyone," I call out.

We're greeted with a few waves, but for the most part, our arrival is lost in the commotion of the room as people pull folding chairs from the closet and voices echo off the wooden floors in all directions.

I set my plate of strawberries on the buffet table in the corner.

"Oh, good. The last of the stragglers have arrived," Shelia Gibson says.

"Great, I'm starving." Edna Plum makes a beeline for the food, and a few ladies join her while the rest of us continue setting up chairs in a big circle.

Mrs. Hayward, the retired high school science teacher, raises an eyebrow at Edna. "Didn't you spend all day at the restaurant? You didn't eat? You own the dang place."

"Oh my gosh, who brought these sweet and sour meatballs? I love you," my friend Regina gushes.

Honey nods her agreement. "Personally, I'm here for the cheese."

"Can you believe this one? I fell in love so hard." Regina grabs my elbow. She is already bouncing out of her skin, ready to talk about the book.

I laugh. "I feel like you say that every time."

Regina's a little older than I am, but she's one of the few people here who is also under the age of forty. She loves this book club just as much as I do. Plus, as a single mom, she doesn't get out with other adults much.

"Guilty. I can't help it. I love them all. I'm sure I'll love yours, too, if you ever let me read it." She bumps me with her hip.

I hesitate before saying, "I might actually take you up on that this time."

"Oooh, yes. Do." Her eyes widen with her smile.

"I should warn you, my professor is definitely not a fan of my writing."

"Pfft. What does he know? Send it my way. Pretty please?"

"I'll think about it. No promises."

"That's what you always say. One of these days I'm going to wear you down and pry those pages away from you"

I grab a small paper plate and pile it high with pretzels, fruit, pickles, crackers, and anything else that doesn't come from a cow. Then I wrap a stack of cookies that are labeled as dairy-free in a napkin.

"Bless your heart, I don't know how you manage to eat all of that and keep your tiny little figure." I don't need to turn around to recognize Shelia Gibson's voice. It's lived in my head rent-free since the morning she found me in her house. She's a master at the southern art of making something sound like a compliment when it's really an insult. Or maybe it's my imagination and she's only trying to make polite conversation, but the way she paused slightly before the word "tiny" makes my insides tighten. I'm convinced everyone nearby understands her implication that real women have the curves I never will.

I lift a hand to rub the Tinker Bell tattoo on the back of my neck. People have used words like *frail* or *lithe* to talk about me for as long as I can remember. I know I have no control over what other women say or the fact that I stopped growing when I hit the fifth grade, but accepting my body doesn't always come as easily for me when I'm cornered by yet another judgmental comment.

People have always called me Tinker Bell both behind my back and to my face. When you're small, people think they can say whatever they want to you and it's supposed to bounce right off. It used to bother me a lot more, until I realized Tinker Bell is kind of a badass. Eventually, I learned to embrace the nickname. I'm sure Shelia has plenty of feelings about my tattoo as well. I know she hates the sleeves covering Jake's arms. Shelia's really good at taking things that have nothing to do with her and getting offended by them.

"What I wouldn't give," she says, plucking a handful of grapes from the fruit tray with her perfectly manicured nails. The cool way her eyes scan over me leaves little doubt about her true feelings.

At least I know she won't be staying long. She never does. Shelia Gibson wouldn't be caught dead reading what she considers to be smut. Although I have my suspicions she reads the books in private, she only comes to the first half of each meeting, then she makes a big fuss about leaving before the discussion heats up. I assume she's mostly here to get the latest gossip and steal a few recipes. Her husband, Ward, is even more uptight. Honey and I have a working theory that he's the one who got Spread Those Pages removed from the library. I have no idea how the two of them produced Jake. Jacob Gibson might be a nerd, but he also has a reputation for getting around. I've heard plenty of stories from the girls we went to school with. Not that I care. He can sleep with whomever he wants.

"I suppose you're delighted you and Jacob will be spending a lot of time together this spring." Shelia raises her eyebrows while she nibbles a cracker. Then she brushes the crumbs from her hands onto a tissue she pulls from the pocket of her practical elastic-waist khakis.

"Not particularly, if I'm being honest. But there's a lot to do now that Danielle is getting married, so we'll work together and get it done." I shrug. Shelia already knows how much work we have ahead of us since the wedding is literally in her back yard.

"I'm sure you will," Shelia says, turning her back to me and taking another small cluster of grapes to add to her plate.

Danielle has always pictured getting married on that pier, and Shelia seems thrilled for the opportunity to host the social event of the year on her property. Although, I expect she's more than a little chagrinned that it wasn't Jake Danielle chose. She has already made it clear she isn't happy about the fact that her son is being "snubbed" by the groom and will be forced to stand with the women instead.

Of course, to anyone capable of rational thought, it makes perfect sense for Jake to stand with his best friend at her wedding. Jake and I are Danielle's co-maids of honor. Well, I'm the maid of honor. He's whatever you're supposed to call a dude in that position. I've started calling him the "male man of honor," and it's catching on because it made Honey laugh. Now she's doing it, too. Jake has too much respect for his elderly neighbor to say anything, but I can see how much he hates it when we call him that. Which is exactly what makes it hilarious. Shelia finds it "unbelievable we would emasculate her son so publicly." She's said so multiple times.

I hate that my hand is shaking as I pop a berry into my mouth, but Shelia has always had an uncanny way of cutting straight to the center of my insecurities. Her eyes scan everyone constantly, as if she's looking for your weaknesses so she can home in and point them out in front of everyone. It's like everything she says to me has a double meaning. I'm not even sure she does it on purpose, but I've been watching her do the same thing to her son and the rest of our friends for our entire lives.

"I liked this book, but I thought it could use a little more spice." We hear Honey's throaty voice carry over all the other chatter in the room as she starts critiquing this month's read. Although, it's not actually a critique because she says the same thing about every single book. I'm not even sure she reads them thoroughly enough to talk about the plot. She probably just skims the pages until she finds a sex scene.

Since the discussion is starting, Shelia is done with us. "Well, ladies, that's my cue to leave. Donna, the macaroni salad is excellent. Regina, please give my regards to little Emily."

We wave our goodbyes. A few women exchange pointed looks with each other when she finally leaves. Everyone's nice enough not to say anything out loud, but I have a feeling more than one person in this room is thinking the same thing I am. *Good riddance.*

"Well then," Edna Plum says, "I guess it's time to—"

"Spread! Those! Pages!" We all chant the name of our group to officially open the meeting. We go around the circle to share our thoughts, but my heart's not in it because Shelia and Ratnick's comments are still swirling in my head. I'm furious they have the power to get to me this much. I refuse to give them any more control.

By the time I get home, I'm worked up enough to gather my courage for the few minutes it takes to send off an email to Regina with my story attached.

Hey, Girl! This is what I'm working on. It's a futuristic dystopian romance set in a matriarchal society. I really would appreciate your thoughts because you always have such insightful comments at book club. If you hate it, let's pretend I never sent this. -A

I need to keep myself busy so I won't overthink what I've just done. Sharing stories with strangers online is no problem. But there's nothing that makes me more uncomfortable than exposing my work to people I know in real life.

I sigh and open a new file to do my actual job.

After crafting this week's newsletter to my readers and making a gif for my social media, I close my laptop and head to my closet. I try on three dresses, jeans, and a faux leather skirt, but I still have no idea what to wear to Danielle's bachelorette party. I shoot off a text to my group chat with Danielle and Regina.

Me: *What's everyone wearing to Danielle's last hurrah as a single woman?*

Regina: *Thinking a sweater dress with boots and tights. Or a dressy top with leggings. P.S. Got your email. Can't wait to read it!*

Danielle: *You sent your new story to Regina and not me?! No fair. Give up the goods, woman. I want a turn.*

Danielle: *And leggings and a cute sweater for me too, probably.*

Me: *Sweet. Sounds like that's the uniform.*

Danielle: *Don't think I didn't notice the deflection. I WILL read that story. But yep. That's the uniform. Except Jake. I doubt we could get our Male Man to agree. But he's never backed down from a dare, so maybe we should try? Haha.*

Me: *That gives me an idea.*

Regina: *Uh-oh. I can only imagine what this involves. I've heard some scary things about your prank war. Remind me to never get on your bad side.*

I text back a devil face emoji and laugh because, just like that, I know exactly what Jake's going to be wearing to this party. I pull my laptop out again to place a quick order.

Chapter 4

Jake

I grab the microphone and strut along the stage, a tiny dong flapping over my bare chest while I belt out an off-key version of Elton John's *Goodbye Yellow Brick Road* to my small audience. Danielle screams and claps from her table in the front row while Alice shifts her chair to give me her back. Thanks to her, I'm giving this epic performance while wearing blue shorts, a vest, and a visor with "I deliver this package" printed in bold letters across the front.

Danielle has a soft spot for karaoke night. She wanted to have her bachelorette party at Brew-Ha-Ha, North Bay's only coffee shop/comedy club/karaoke lounge. Normally, this place closes at ten, but they offered to keep the doors open late for us. Mercifully, those of us in Danielle's bridal party and her family are the only people here. I'm taking my turn on stage while she, Alice, Ms. Honey, and Danielle's mom, Ms. Heather, watch from below. Regina was here for a while, but she had to leave early to relieve the babysitter. Edna Plum from The Blue Crab restaurant across the street also stopped by, but she needed to get back to close the kitchen.

When Alice showed up tonight, she told me I had a choice. I could don this "sexy mailman" costume for the entirety of this party, or she would think of a bigger prank to pull on the wedding day. Obviously, I had to take the dare. If Alice got even a whiff of hesitation on my part, she'd think she won this round, and I simply can't allow that. So, I gave her my brightest smile and said, "Challenge accepted." Then I pulled her plastic penis-shaped necklace right over her head and put it around my neck.

Along with their necklaces, all the women in our group are wearing tiaras that flash the word "party" in bright pink lights, and they've distributed some to the staff as well. At least my mailman visor spares me from having to wear one of those, and Mike and his baseball buddies aren't here to witness this. Although with all the selfies the ladies are taking, I'm sure there will be plenty of photographic evidence online before I even get off the stage.

As I wrap up what I hope is my final song of the night, Honey suggests cutting into the homemade cake she brought. It's decorated with paper printouts of eggplants and peaches taped to toothpicks.

"I decided to keep it classy," she tells her granddaughter.

"And we all thank you for that." Ms. Heather laughs.

After Danielle gets her slice, I pull her aside and hand her the small blue gift bag I brought with me. "Hey, Dan-Dan. I have something for you. Sorry it's late. I was hoping to finish this before the bridal shower last weekend, but obviously that didn't happen."

"Is this what I think it is?"

I nod as Danielle opens the card I taped to the outside of the bag. There's a huge smile on her face as she holds the rectangular paper close to her chest.

"I'm keeping this forever. Thanks, Jake. This is why you're my favorite male man," she says.

I roll my eyes, but I knew she'd like it. Not every bride would be excited to receive a gag gift in the form of a fake check for one thousand dollars, made out to Captain Fartpants, but Danielle is. It's an inside joke, thanks to a dare she issued that got me in trouble when we were young.

"'You're welcome," I tell her. Then I raise my voice. "And 'honor attendant' is the correct term for when your maid of honor is a man, in case anyone was wondering," I announce to the room for probably the fiftieth time.

"We weren't," Alice deadpans.

Unfortunately, no one in Danielle's wedding party is receptive to the "Call Jake an Honor Attendant" memo, and now Danielle's family and all our mutual childhood friends are calling me by the very redundant phrase "Male Man of Honor," or "male man" for short.

I ignore Alice and point to the gift bag in Danielle's hand. "Don't worry, there's a real gift, too."

She claps giddily before digging through the tissue paper until she finds the frame.

"Jake!" Danielle gasps. "It's perfect."

"I'm glad you like it." I shrug like it was nothing, but the hand-drawn sketch of the pier painted over with watercolors took me longer than I would like to admit.

"I love it," she whispers.

It takes everything in me to hold back the words *I love you*. We've always said that to each other and, while it's completely platonic now and I'm mostly over the rejection I got from her last year, it's still true. But I don't want to make it weird.

"Mike will love it, too. Thank you, Jake. You really are the best male man I could ever ask for." She winks.

I tip my visor at her. "I do what I can."

My best friend is a woman, and Danielle's getting married to a professional baseball player. My job is to be supportive, even though their relationship started the day she walked out of the one and only date she ever had with me so she could go home with him. I no longer have any romantic feelings for her, but the bruise to my ego is taking a while to heal.

We worked it out. Mike is actually a great guy. Even I can see he was the better choice for her, but that doesn't make this wedding business any less complicated. I'm one of the two friends she chose to stand by her side at the altar. Or, in this case, the pier in my parents' backyard. I'd do anything for Danielle, including make an ass out of myself at this party, but her wedding is changing everything between us, and it doesn't matter how cool of a guy Mike is, losing a lot of the threads that have tied me to my best friend since before we could walk is unnerving. Too bad the only other person who can understand is the reason I'm wearing this ridiculous get-up.

"That's one beautiful drawing." Ms. Honey smacks the middle of my back and raises a margarita glass to toast me. Then we all take our seats for another round.

They don't serve alcohol at Brew-Ha-Ha, but on special occasions they let us BYOB, so there are two sports drink coolers taking up the table next to ours. One is filled with sangria and the other holds margaritas, the drinks Ms. Honey is famous for bringing to any and all celebratory events. I brought a six-pack, but I stopped after my second beer.

"Jake, are you sleeping over at our place tonight, too?" Danielle asks me from across the table where she and Alice are planning which movie they'll watch when they get back to Honey's.

"Don't back out on account of me." Alice's eyes narrow, and she stares me down as she talks over the rim of her mug. She has switched to coffee, presumably so she can be the one to take care of Danielle and Ms. Honey tonight if they get a little too wild.

Alice *really* doesn't like me. I don't know what I did to make her hate me so much in the first place. But our unspoken feud has gotten worse this year, since my parents kicked her out. Lousy, Dan-Dan and I were like the Three Musketeers growing up, but these days she truly seems to have it out for me.

"Don't flatter yourself, sweetheart. You don't tend to register in my thoughts." I scoot my chair a few inches further away from her.

Okay, so sometimes I egg her on a bit.

I pull out my phone to check the time, and there's an alert from my weather app. The forecast calls for a tropical storm to come up the coast later this week. It's hitting the Atlantic side of Florida now. It will be a few days before it gets up to us in Virginia. The news is reporting it should blow through and be out of here in time for the wedding, but I know Danielle is stressing about the weather, too.

There's a lot of girl talk happening around me. I'm trying not to hear too much of their conversation and pretend to give my phone my full attention, but pieces of the chatter are floating through against my will. It's hard not to listen, even as I actively try not to.

"What do you mean you aren't wearing underwear?" Danielle asks.

I keep my head down, but I sneak a quick glance at them. Danielle stares at Alice, her eyes huge under her flashing tiara. It's like they are trying to torture me.

"Who wears underwear with leggings?" Alice scoffs.

I didn't hear how they got on the topic of how to avoid visible panty lines, but this is knowledge I did not ask for, and I swear my brain is short-circuiting as it registers there is only one thin layer of fabric covering Lousy's lap. I look up. I can't even pretend I'm not watching them anymore.

There's an extended pause before Danielle says, "Um, everyone. Or so I thought."

Alice shakes her head and Danielle's mouth hangs open for a second before she asks, "Are you telling me this is a common thing? What about…*discharge*? And what happens if you get your period? What if you sneeze and pee a little?"

This is getting to be way too much for me. I want to go home.

"Babe, it sounds like someone might need to do some pelvic floor exercises. Besides, they have that little bit of extra padding in the crotch for a reason. But maybe bring the noise level down a smidge." Alice's gaze slides over to me, but I look back at my phone.

"That extra fabric is called the gusset. We all gotta let the old girl air out sometimes, Sugar," Honey interjects, fanning her own lap. Alice chokes on her coffee and sputters it down the front of her shirt, which gives me a perfect opportunity.

"I think that's my cue to call it a night." I stand and give them a wave before I turn to head out.

"Oh, Jake. Don't leave because of us. Sorry. We'll stop being inappropriate," Danielle says.

"Speak for yourself," Honey tells her.

Danielle stands to give me a quick hug because I really am leaving, then she turns her attention back to Honey. "Please never say the word *gusset* ever again." She puts her hands over her ears and pretends to gag. She does that a lot around Honey. "I'm never going to be able to erase that from my brain, and you're scaring my friends away."

"That's not why I'm leaving," I say, even though it sort of is.

"No one cares," Alice tells me as she pulls Danielle's hands back down. "But before we break up the band tonight, what's the plan for this week?"

Danielle pivots right into assertive bride mode. "We're coming down the home stretch on the wedding tasks. Only a week away now. Eek! Can you believe it?" She hops on her toes. "There are only a few more last-minute errands to run. Can we all meet up on Tuesday morning since Alice doesn't have class? I'm hoping to get as much done as we can at the beginning of the week before the weather changes."

"Sure thing," Alice says. "I should be able to handle that after I get my dad situated."

"Yeah, I'll be there, too," I promise before I'm finally allowed to leave. I have to be up early so I can do the pre-wedding thing again with the guys in the morning. I can't wait until this week is over.

Chapter 5

Jake

There aren't many places in North Bay to take a sober dude for his bachelor party. I was roped into planning this event because I'm the only townie. Mike's teammates don't have as many local connections. Or at least that's the excuse they used to get out of doing any of the legwork. I convinced Chuck, The Blue Crab's seafood supplier, to let us charter his boat and go fishing on the bay for the day. It seemed like a good idea at the time. But after only four hours of sleep thanks to Danielle's karaoke night, I'm stuck on this boat bright and early with a killer headache, trying to find a way to celebrate with Mike, Jordan, and Rodriguez without any alcohol. Just me, three pro athletes, and Chuck, with several hours to kill while we float on choppy water. And I thought girls' night was bad.

Chuck is driving the boat and otherwise completely ignoring us, not that I blame him. These other guys all work and travel together, so there's an easy flow to the conversations among them. I'm definitely the odd man out. They're making a strong effort to include me, which is nice of them, but the stunted attempts at small talk are just making it more awkward. Obviously, the male man of honor thing is going really well.

"So, Gibson, Mike says you're an artist?" To his credit, Jordan is really trying. But the way he's forcing this makes it feel like a bad first date.

"Yeah. It's a side gig, mostly. I also manage a few of my uncle's rental properties."

I take a sip of Coke from the plastic bottle in my hand. None of these guys were brought up in the South, so I brought peanuts and Coke for them to try. Danielle and I grew up drinking these every summer. Judging by the way all of theirs are sitting untouched, peanuts floating in brown liquid, I'm not sure they appreciate the taste of Southern charm the way I hoped they would. I'm trying to hold my own, but it's hard to do when I'm surrounded by dudes who are all in great physical condition and at the top of their game. I'm almost six feet tall and I try to stay in shape, but they still each have at least three inches and thirty pounds of muscle over me.

"What kind of stuff do you draw?"

"Mostly fantasy, some sci-fi." I try to stand my ground and say it with confidence, but I can hear my dad's voice telling me how absurd it is to be a college drop-out, living at home, unemployed, and sitting around drawing cartoons.

"Oh, sweet. Can you draw a dragon?"

"Uh, yeah, sure."

I'm not really unemployed because I do have a stream of income coming in. But Dad will never consider *self-employed artist and part-time property manager for Uncle Tim* to be a real job.

I swallow. It might not be the same as being a professional ball player, but people like my art well enough to pay for it. I've sold a few pieces through social media and done some commissions. Yesterday, a woman emailed me about painting a mural in her son's bedroom. That's something, right?

Jordan seems to agree. At least he's making an effort.

"You play first base, right?" I ask, trying to reciprocate even though I already know his position. Everyone in North Bay is familiar with the team's roster.

"Yeah. Going into my third year with The Blue Crabs. Although, if I can't find a new roommate soon, I might need to give up baseball and ask Chuck over there if he'll hire me." He's kidding about quitting baseball, but I think he's serious about needing a roommate. Minor league players don't make a ton of money. Jordan and Mike used to live together, but now that Mike's marrying Danielle and they're buying Ms. Honey's house, Mike's obviously out of the picture.

"Rodriguez doesn't want to live with you?" I ask, pointing my soda in his teammate's direction.

"No offense, man. But we spend enough time together as it is. I like living alone," Rodriguez chimes in before taking a sip of his bottle. "You know, this isn't half bad, Gibson," he says, giving the soda and peanuts another chance.

"I guess I'm just not a huge fan of stuff floating in my drinks," Mike says. "Danielle finally got me to try bubble tea, and I couldn't get on board with that either."

"Oh, yeah? This is my surprised face. Your picky ass doesn't like anything the first time you try it. The whole reason we're all here today is because you were such a crybaby about the steamed crabs," Jordan ribs him, putting on a fake whiny voice. "Excuse me? Waitress? Can you help me? The mean little crab gave me an ouchie, and now I'm scared to eat him."

"I remember it differently," Mike deadpans. Then he raises his soda bottle. "I want to make a toast. I'm really glad all of you are here. Rodriguez, here's to you for sharing our rookie season together, and for always having my back, even when I ditched you at the charity event to drive Danielle home."

I look at my feet because my memory of that night is not nearly as fond as Mike's.

He continues his toast. "Jordan, you're the best friend I've ever had. I love you, man." Finally, he gets to me. "Jake, I know we've had our differences, but I'm glad you're here. Danielle considers you family, which means you're my brother now, too. Thanks for putting this together."

"Uh, sure," I mumble.

Mike raises his bottle and we all take a sip from our own, then Mike and Rodriguez step away to check the lines.

I turn to Jordan. "Is he always that sappy?"

He shrugs. "Nothing wrong with a man being honest. But no, he wasn't always that open about stuff. Therapy, bro. It works."

"Maybe I should try it sometime," I say, only half-kidding.

He chuckles. "You and me both."

I like Jordan. "Do you really need a roommate?"

"Why? You interested?"

"Actually, yeah. As long as you're okay with a dog."

"For real? Okay, put your number in my phone and we can plan for you to see the place this week."

"I can already tell you, I'm in."

I've already seen his apartment once, but it wouldn't matter anyway. I'll sleep in a closet if it gets me out of my parents' house.

He hands me his phone, and I start sending a text to myself. While I'm typing, a new message comes through. It's from someone he has listed as Sea Shell, who I can only assume is Shelley Miller, Mike's sister. They definitely seemed into each other when she was go-karting with us last year. All I know is that this text is absolutely not safe for work, and I'm staying the hell out of it.

But reading Shelley's spicy invitation to Jordan makes someone else pop into my head, uninvited. I shake my head, trying to ditch the image of Alice looking at me over her coffee mug and the knowledge I shouldn't have about her underwear preferences. Or lack thereof.

I hand the phone back to Jordan, and when he realizes I must have seen the text, he locks eyes with me.

"I know how it looks, but it's really not like that," he insists. "We text sometimes, and we hang out when she's here. But that's all. I wouldn't mess with Shelley behind Mike's back." Jordan pockets his phone again.

I give a small nod and take a long sip of my drink, keeping my mouth shut to let him know that I have no intention of ratting him out. Jordan and Shelley hooking up might throw a wrench in things as far as her brother is concerned, but I doubt anyone else would care.

Alice and I hooking up, on the other hand, would throw a grenade on everything. Even if we could stand to be around each other for more than five minutes at a time, which we definitely can't, it would still be a terrible idea. My parents would probably disown me, plus it could screw up both our friendships with Danielle. Unfortunately, knowing it can't happen is exactly what makes the thought of it so hot, and now I can't get her out of my head.

There's a pull on one of the lines hanging off the other side of the boat, and Rodriguez starts to reel it in.

"Sweet, we might actually catch something today." After a few minutes of struggle, he hoists a rockfish onto the deck, and we take a few photos with it.

Two hours later, we send Mike home with a cooler full of fresh fish and a quick lesson from Chuck on how to clean them. I reassure him Danielle can walk him through the process if he forgets.

"You boys cut it close with this one. Got your group out just in the nick of time," Chuck says when I hand over the tip our group collected for him. He pockets the cash and cranes his neck toward the sky. "Storms will be rolling in earlier than they're calling for, I'd bet money on it."

"News said we should have until Wednesday," I offer.

He shakes his head. "No way this one will wait that long. You'll see."

I wouldn't bet against Chuck. At least if the storm does come early, it'll give us more time to clean up before the wedding on Saturday.

Chapter 6

Alice

Tuesday morning I rush through the kitchen unpacking groceries. The store was a madhouse. With the storms on the way, it seems like everyone in town had the same idea to stock up on supplies.

"Okay," I call out to my dad. "I got canned ravioli and stuff to make peanut butter and jelly sandwiches. I also ran by the pharmacy and picked up the refill on your meds. And I wiped down the bathroom this morning. We're good on toilet paper." The last thing I want is for us to be stuck without his blood pressure medication or in a filthy house for days with no water or electricity. "Do you need anything else?" I say, coming into the living room.

"You get those chips I like?" Dad asks. He seems more tired lately than usual, and his beard has grown out to the point of looking scraggly.

"There are two bags in the pantry."

"Good."

"Okay, I'm heading over to Danielle's. We have errands to run for the wedding."

He acknowledges me with a grunt and a nod, and I pause for just a second to run through my mental checklist, making sure I've done everything here before turning to leave.

The entire bridal party is waiting on me by the time I pull Bertie up to Honey's house. I close my eyes and swallow the lump in my throat. I hate being late. It feels like I'm being irresponsible and disappointing everyone, even though I don't think my friends see it that way. I tell myself it's only ten minutes after nine, so I'm not *that* late. But I hate letting people down, especially my bestie when I have official MOH duties to fulfill.

"I'm so sorry," I say to Danielle. "It took longer than expected to make sure my dad had what he needed this morning."

"No worries. Glad you're here. There's so much to do, and this weather they're calling for sounds pretty intense. I want to try to get as much done this morning as we can so we can all be home before the rain rolls in."

From the look of the darkening clouds and the way the wind is picking up, we probably don't have long. Danielle continues, "We should split up. Obviously, I need to be the one to go to the final dress fitting. Maybe you can go to the bakery? They said they'd have the cupcakes ready for me early, and they should still be fine for the wedding."

"Of course."

She hesitates. "Um, the thing is, the bakery is kind of a two-person job. I'd feel better if Jake went with you."

"Truly not wanted or necessary. I'll be fine," I promise.

She waves Jake over anyway. "There are a ton of cupcakes. Plus, I don't want you to have to drive alone if the storm comes."

I try to contain my groan.

"You're lucky we're not allowed to say no to the bride," Jake tells her without looking at me. "Because a road trip with this one is pretty high on the list of things that might kill me." He points in my direction.

Danielle shrugs, not taking the bait from him either. "I think there's a pretty high likelihood you'll both survive."

"Fine, but I'm driving," Jake insists. "At least cupcake pickup seems very within my wheelhouse. Dress fitting, not so much." Then he turns to me. "Nice of you to finally join us, Louse. Oversleep the alarm, or just forget how to read a clock? We can get you one with big, bright numbers if you still aren't sure what the big hands and the little hands mean."

"Shut up. I got stuck at the store," I grind out.

Jake laughs. "Stuck. Right. Trying to push again when the door said pull?"

"It was *one* time," I say through gritted teeth, my cheeks hot.

"Okay, you two. Play nice," Danielle intervenes, still smiling. "Can I trust you to control your tempers long enough to ride out to the bakery and back?" If she's annoyed with our bickering, she's not showing it. She's too excited about the wedding to let anything bring down her mood. Nothing will get to her today. Not the storm, and definitely not me fighting with Jake.

"Fine," I agree. "But if we're going all the way to Marnock, we need to get a move on."

He nods. "Yeah. I want to get this over with."

At least we agree on one thing.

I stare out the window, not interested in engaging with Jake, watching as more dark clouds gather overhead. Thunder crackles in the distance, but thankfully the rain holds off for our drive, and we arrive at the Sweet Things bakery unscathed.

As I open the door, a chime sounds to announce our arrival. I let the door swing closed on Jake behind me. Leaving him in my dust, I smile at the only employee here.

"Hi, we have an order to pick up for the Daniels-Miller wedding," I tell her, just as Jake comes up and flicks my shoulder. I turn to stick my tongue out at him.

"Thank goodness," the woman behind the counter says. "I was hoping you'd get here soon. I just sent the rest of the staff home, and I'm about to close up early. This storm is set to be a real doozy. I'm Margot. If you'll both follow me. The order is all boxed up and ready to go."

Margot leads the way toward the back of the bakery. Jake steps around me, so he is the first to follow her into the kitchen area. Then he stops short, so I walk into him.

"Very mature," I mutter.

He shrugs. "I know you are, but what am I?"

"So, you admit I'm the mature one?"

Now he's the one to stick out his tongue. Margot's eyes move back and forth between us like she's assessing if she can trust us with her creations. I snarl at Jake and turn my attention to the cupcakes in boxes on the counter.

I peek into the boxes through their plastic windows. "Oh, wow. These are gorgeous."

Half of the cupcakes are piled high with icing that looks like it has been painted with watercolors in different shades of blue, and there is a tiny bit of gold dust making them shimmer. The other half holds small sculptures of blue crabs crafted out of fondant.

Margot beams and puts one hand over her heart. "Thank you. I love them, too. Ms. Daniels had a very specific vision, and I'm so glad we could execute it for her here at Sweet Things."

We each carry two stacked boxes and arrange them in the back of the car, then Jake heads back inside for the rest. We thank Margot and hurry to get back on the road as quickly as we can. No sooner than we shut the doors and buckle our seatbelts, the sky unleashes. Sheets of rain pound the windshield of Jake's Outlander.

"It's coming from the direction of home. They're probably getting the worst of it in North Bay now," Jake says as he leans forward, trying to see the road. He clicks on the high beams, but they don't help. The rain is already coming down so hard we can't even see the hood of the car we are riding in, let alone anything else. Thankfully, we're the only ones on the road. I guess everyone else was smart enough to stay home when we all knew this mess was headed our way.

"Should we pull over and wait it out?" I ask.

"Maybe? But the storms are supposed to last for a while. If it gets worse, we're going to need a better shelter than the car."

"Is it supposed to get worse than this?" I swallow, rubbing my palm on the hem of my shorts.

Jake shrugs. "It's a tropical storm, Louse. The news said it might even turn into a hurricane by the time it gets to us. This is only the beginning."

That does not make me feel better. I'm keeping it together for now because I refuse to let him see me fall apart, but I hate storms.

I reach out to the screen on Jake's dashboard to disconnect his phone so we can hear the local news, but he pulls my hand down and places it on my lap. "Don't touch a man's car without his permission."

"Oh, I can't touch your radio, but it's fine for you to leave tuna under my seat?" I snap.

That infuriating smirk is back on his face. "I'm glad you understand the rules."

I give up. I fold my arms, trying to calm the flips my stomach is doing. A clap of thunder booms far too close for comfort and causes me to jolt. Jake looks briefly in my direction, then he changes the radio dials until we hear an announcer talking about the storm.

"North Bay residents are advised to stay off the roads if at all possible. The bridge is closed due to falling debris. Conditions have been deemed impassible." When the announcement is finished, a pop song starts playing that is way too peppy to match the dread I'm feeling.

"Shit," Jake mutters under his breath, echoing my own thoughts. He pulls into a driveway to turn the car around.

We're silent as he drives the streets of Marnock. The windshield wipers rock back and forth in a steady rhythm that competes with the song. There's only one main road that leads into North Bay. We aren't getting home until they open the bridge. The only other way we could get there would be by boat, and that clearly is not happening in this weather.

The music cuts abruptly and both our phones buzz at the same time. A shrill alarm sounds on the radio before switching back to the announcer's voice. "This is an emergency alert. A tornado watch has been issued for the Northern Neck of Virginia. Residents of North Bay, Marnock, and surrounding areas are advised to stay indoors and remain alert."

The bridge is out. We can't get home. It's pouring down rain. And now there is a freaking tornado? You've got to be kidding me.

I turn to Jake. "What do we do?" My voice waivers.

"It's okay. They said 'watch,' right? The watch only means conditions are possible. A warning would mean there's an actual tornado nearby. We don't need to worry yet. Hopefully, it won't come to that. One of the rentals I'm helping my uncle remodel is a few blocks from here. We're going there."

I try to focus on taking calming breaths while the panic threatens to pull me under. The wind is howling right on the other side of my door. At least Jake has a plan.

It doesn't take long to find the adorable little cottage nestled on a secluded lot along the creek. At least, I think it's adorable from what I can see through the rain. Which, in this downpour, isn't much. But I can make out the yellow siding and overgrown hydrangea bushes flanking a small front porch and the creek that runs behind the house, which is already flowing violently. I hope the water won't rise high enough to flood, because there is nowhere else for us to go.

Jake parks the car in the driveway and reaches into the center console for a garage door opener. When he presses the button nothing happens.

"The power is probably out already. Just stay here," he says.

I don't bother arguing. He steps out into the deluge, and I watch as he is soaked through well before he lets himself into the house through the front door. I rub my hands down my legs, wondering how long I'm supposed to wait until I follow him, but it isn't long until the garage door opens and a sopping wet Jake reappears. He opens the driver's side door. His shirt is drenched and clinging to him, and his hair is plastered to his forehead.

"Yeah. Power is definitely out." He raises his voice over the rain as he pulls the car into the garage. "I had to open it manually."

"You really didn't have to open the garage just to keep me dry. I could have used the front door, too. I'm not afraid to get a little wet."

He looks at me and smirks as he shifts into park. "That's good to know. But I did it for my car. If we leave it outside and a tree branch falls through the windshield, or if it starts hailing soon, a damaged vehicle isn't going to get us back home."

"Right. Of course. That makes sense." Embarrassment heats my cheeks again. Why would I think Jake Gibson was bothering to be chivalrous and trying to keep me out of the rain? This is the same guy who was just flicking me and making me run into him at the bakery. Then again, he did tell me to stay put inside the same car he was trying to protect. Maybe he's less of a jerk during weather-related emergencies.

Jake gets out of the car and reaches into the back seat to grab a hoodie to replace his wet shirt. I mostly look away while he strips the clingy fabric from his body, and I only sort of notice the way his abs ripple and the fact that his chest is smooth when he pulls the hoodie over his head. *Does he shave all his body hair?* That's a great example of a thought I will not be having while I'm stuck here alone with this man.

"You planning to sit in the car all day, or can I get a little help out here?" Jake calls.

By the time we work together to close the door to the small garage, with the car now safely inside, the sky is so dark it looks like we've teleported time zones. It could be the middle of the night instead of ten-thirty in the morning. There are two small windows in the cement walls, but still barely any light.

I follow Jake into the house, through a dark kitchen, and into the living space while thunder booms so loudly it feels like the house is shaking. Jake tries the light switch in the living room, but of course nothing happens. The power is out for sure. Great. There are drop cloths thrown over the furniture, and a ladder is propped up against the wall. A thin layer of drywall dust coats most of the surfaces, and shadows conceal the corners, giving the place a haunted house vibe I could do without under the circumstances.

"Are we really any safer in the middle of a construction site?" I ask.

His nostrils flare. "My apologies, but all the five-star hotels were fully booked."

Jake hangs his wet shirt over the back of a wooden dining chair and gets to work taking the cover off the sofa. I try to make myself useful by turning on the flashlight on my phone and searching for whatever items might be helpful. I find a few candles and a package of matches on a shelf in the kitchen. Then I wander upstairs.

It's a Cape Cod-style house, and there are two rooms at the top of the steps with a small bathroom between them. One of the rooms is completely empty, except for another ladder and some peeled wallpaper on the floor. The other contains a dusty antique dresser and a brass bed with a bare mattress. One bed. No sheets. No blankets. Awesome. At least there's also a sofa downstairs.

I pull out my phone again, and a new prairie dog photo makes me feel a little better. I save it, then I send texts to my dad and Danielle to tell them we're okay, but we will need to stay in Marnock to ride out the storm. I omit Jake's name in my text to my dad. He probably assumes by "we" I mean Danielle and I are together, and I have no intention of elaborating.

Dad only sends a thumbs-up in response, but Danielle texts back immediately.

Danielle: *Glad you're safe. All's well here, too. Please don't destroy each other. I'm rather fond of you both.*
Me: *No promises.*

Once we light a candle and scan our surroundings, Jake and I are left staring at each other in the middle of the dusty living room.

"What now?"

He turns up his palms. "I guess we just…wait?"

Jake takes a seat on the couch and makes a sweeping motion with his hand that passes as an invitation for me to sit next to him. He puts his elbows on his knees and bounces his legs.

"Aww, are you scared of the storm?" I tease him. Although, truthfully, I'm getting more and more nervous myself.

It's been a while since our area has been hit with one this big. Two summers ago we had a few bad storms roll through, and it took weeks for North Bay to recover from the damage. I remember all the downed trees, scary winds, and rising water. The thought of a tornado added to all of that is terrifying. Plus, I'm worried about my dad riding this out alone. Not to mention what we would do if there is any significant damage to the house. I don't know how we'd be able to scrounge up the deductible for the home owner's insurance, assuming they would even decide to cover it. Can't these kinds of things be considered an "act of God?" What if our coverage is denied? Then what will we do? *In through your nose, out through your mouth.* I try to focus on my breath and not make my spiraling too obvious to my temporary housemate.

Jake glares and shakes his head.

"If you must know, I was thinking about things we need to do," he says, one knee still bouncing. "I don't know how long we'll be stuck here, but with the bridge out and the roads flooding, it's going to be a least tonight. There's no electricity, and this house is on well water with an electric pump. So, if you want to, you know, not die, we probably need to figure out the water situation first."

Seeing Jake be this serious is sobering. He's usually so carefree about everything.

"I saw some bottled water in the kitchen," I offer. "So, we've got drinking water."

"Good. That's good." He nods, stoic.

"But the pantry wasn't very well-stocked. I'm not sure we have any food." I chew my bottom lip.

Jake laughs.

"Are you actually laughing at me right now because I'm concerned we might starve? God, you're such a di—"

"Calm down," he interrupts. "I'm laughing because, apparently, you forgot what brought us here. We have plenty of food. There's an entire trunkload of cupcakes in the garage. We obviously won't starve. But we might have to buy Danielle and Mike apology cupcakes to make up for the ones we eat."

"Do you ever find it works well to tell people to calm down in the middle of an actual crisis?" I snap.

Those cupcakes aren't going to be dairy-free. This does not bode well for my stomach. I get along with dairy even less than I get along with Jake.

He closes his eyes and inhales through his nose. I can tell he's trying to bite back whatever it is he really wants to say to me. After a beat, his face softens a little. "I didn't intend to offend you. I'm sorry. I'll try not to do it again."

In fairness, I could probably also make more of an effort. I *was* in the middle of calling him names when he said that.

"Whatever."

I dump the contents of my purse onto the dusty coffee table and start sorting, picking out anything that I think might be useful. I swear I threw a portable charger in here before class last week. I chew the inside of my cheek as I dig through the side pockets until I find it.

"Hey," Jake says, causing me to look over at him. "Everything's going to be fine."

Chapter 7

Jake

I need her to believe me because the last thing I want to deal with right now is a hysterical version of Alice Caulfield. Besides, everything really is going to be fine. Relatively. Sure, I'm trapped in a dilapidated two-bedroom cottage without electricity or running water, and I'm here with the one woman on Earth who wants to be stuck with me even less than I want to be stuck with her. But we have a roof, enough to drink, and the sky is pouring out plenty of additional water. Plus, there are sixteen dozen cupcakes in the back of my car.

The next few days might not be pleasant, but as long as the creek doesn't flood into the house, we can figure out a way to make this work. I hope.

Alice looks nervous, and she's clearly upset about something other than the obvious issue of our current situation. I doubt she'll tell me what it is. I might not be her favorite person, but I need her to know she can trust me tonight. I'll have to pull back on the usual barbs.

"I'm going to look around for a bucket."

I pop up from the couch and squint my way into the kitchen, feeling my hand along the wall because, with only one small window above the sink and the storm still raging, it's hard to make out much in this room. It doesn't take long to find a bucket under the sink, but Alice was right, the only food I see in here is an open bag of rice. Looks like we'll be breaking into those wedding cupcakes for sure.

I might also have some jerky or something in my car, but I doubt Alice will be willing to eat it. Ever since our class watched a documentary about the intelligence of whales in the fifth grade, she's been an on-and-off vegetarian. I don't know if she's eating meat right now.

I know people are starting to worry about us, so I send Danielle a text to check-in. I need to call my parents, too, but that can wait until I have the energy to deal with them.

Me: *Stuck in Marnock at Uncle Tim's. We're okay, but have no food. There may be fewer cupcakes in these boxes when we get back. Sorry. You good?*

She writes back quickly.

Dan-Dan: *All good here. Zero worries about the cupcakes. Do what you need to do. Stay dry and play nice. I need both of my besties back in one piece.*

Me: *I'll try. Can't speak for Louse. Turning my phone to airplane mode now. Check back later.*

Then I do switch my phone over to conserve the battery as much as I can. When I find my way back into the living room, Alice is still sitting on the sofa. Her knees are pulled up to her chest, and she's curling in on herself.

"Are we supposed to, you know, *go* in that thing?" She points at the bucket I'm holding.

I bark out a laugh. "Yep."

I have no problem letting her think that for a while. This is my chance to get my revenge for the mailman costume.

She brushes her hand over her face and turns away, trying to hide the fact that she's sniffling.

My resolve crumbles. "Come on, Lousy, I'm not *that* bad. The bucket is for rainwater. We can still use the bathroom like normal, we just have to fill the tank to be able to flush. I didn't mean to make you cry."

Thanks to the candle on the coffee table, I can see her roll her eyes when she faces me again. My own eyes have adjusted enough to the dim lighting to notice that hers are red, and her wet lashes are making her blue irises look even brighter. She's always had those piercing eyes that remind me of the White Walkers from Game of Thrones.

"Shockingly, not everything is about you. Sometimes people have whole entire thoughts in which you play no part at all."

"Fair enough. Guess you're not going to share what's making your eyes leak, then?"

"No. It's nothing." She forces out a little cough.

"It's obviously not nothing, but you also clearly don't want to talk to me about it, so suit yourself. I'm going to grab one of the cupcake boxes. There wasn't much else to eat, unless you want to try to boil rice over a candle."

In the flickering candlelight, I can see the way she chews her lower lip. "I'm not hungry."

She's a liar. I can hear her stomach growling from here.

"Well, I'm starving," I say, as I head out to the garage.

I return with a box and set it on the coffee table in front of her. Careful to keep a comfortable distance between our bodies, I sit down on the sofa and open the box. She doesn't budge.

"Eat, will you?" I take a cupcake for myself and peel off the paper before taking a bite.

"I just don't think we should be eating our friends' wedding cake. That has to be bad luck, and we're in no position to be bringing any more of that upon ourselves."

It's my turn to roll my eyes. "I already texted Dan-Dan about it, and she gave us her blessing. Her exact words were 'zero worries.' It's fine."

She scans the cupcakes.

"Will it make a difference if I tell you these are the vegan ones?"

"What vegan ones?"

"The last two boxes I grabbed from the bakery. They don't have milk in them. Or eggs, if that matters." There's a giant sticker on the back of the box labeling them dairy-free. I turn it so she can see for herself.

"Really?" She seems so surprised, and for some reason the way her voice gets small, as if she doesn't think she deserves them, feels like a punch to my chest.

"You think Danielle was going to serve things at her wedding that her maid of honor couldn't even eat? That was the whole reason she used the bakery all the way out here. She wanted you to have options."

"Oh my God, really?" Her face pales. "I'm the reason we're stuck here?"

Another laugh escapes before I can stop it, and she glares at me. "Sorry Lousy, but it looks that way. It's totally your fault there's a hurricane, and how dare you take out an entire bridge all by yourself?" I shake my head and smile. She's ridiculous. "I didn't realize I was sitting here with Ororo Munroe. You really need to learn how to control your weather manipulation superpower." I don't think she knows who I'm talking about because she only blinks at me. "Storm? From the X-Men?"

"You're going to need to use less nerdy references if you want me to understand you," she chides, but she finally takes a cupcake. The way her eyes flutter closed and she lets out a little moan after the first bite has me needing to look away before I say something stupid.

In any other context, staying overnight in a private creek-side cottage and sharing cupcakes with a woman would seem romantic. With Alice, it's just awkward. We sit silently, side-by-side on the couch, and try not to touch each other. There are a few mumbled "sorry"s when we both try to reach into the box at the same time, and at one point she taps her own face as a signal that I have icing on mine. After I wipe it off with my index finger, we both stare straight ahead at the non-functioning TV for what seems like an infinite amount of time. It's quiet except for the constant pounding of rain on the roof and the occasional clap of thunder, until Alice's phone starts shaking on the table and an alert flashes on the screen. *Tornado warning. Take shelter immediately.*

"Jake." Her eyes are wide. "What's happening?"

I jump up and pull the cushions off the couch, tossing one at her. "We need to get in the tub. Take this."

"What?" She shakes her head, confused as she clutches the cushion.

I reach out and yank her up by the wrist, pulling her with me and carrying two cushions in my other arm. We haul ass down the hallway and I climb into the tub, spreading my legs as much as I can to make space for her, but my body takes up most of the room in a standard-sized tub. She's going to need to sit on me.

"Come here."

Alice doesn't move. It's like she's frozen in place.

"Get in," I urge her again.

She snaps out of her trance and shakes her head. "No. This is insane. I'm not sitting on your lap in the bathroom to hide from a thunderstorm. I'm going back to the couch." It figures the one time she chooses not to be dramatic is now, when it would actually be warranted.

"It's a tornado in the middle of a hurricane. Get in the damn bathtub, Alice. Now."

Maybe it's my tone of voice or maybe it's that I don't usually call her by her real name, but something finally gets through to her enough to make her cooperate. She grunts loudly in protest, but she climbs in and nestles her body on top of my thighs.

"And he says *I* overreact," she mumbles to herself. I don't need to look at her to know she's rolling her eyes again.

The tub is small, and it's not easy for both of us to fit. I lock my arms around her waist, and she piles the cushions on top of us for an extra layer of protection. Then she leans back into my chest. Neither of us speaks for the next few minutes as we listen to the wind howl outside. I feel her flinch every time the thunder booms or a tree branch falls on the roof. She's going to give herself a heart attack being this jumpy. I wrap my arms a little bit tighter around her and hunch over further to whisper into the top of her head.

"You're okay. I've got you. It won't last much longer."

Her hair smells like oranges. She groans like my words are annoying her, and she tries to wriggle out of my grasp, but eventually I feel her relax into me.

The reaction my body has to hers is involuntary.

Chapter 8

Alice

If someone had told me this morning that I'd sit in Jake's lap for almost an hour before the day was over, I would've asked what they were smoking. I hate being trapped here, but I have to admit, he's a much better partner for riding out the storm than I expected. He always seems to have a plan, and even when those plans are stupid—like eating nothing but cupcakes for the foreseeable future and hiding in a bathtub under couch cushions—just knowing there is a plan helps to ease some of my anxiety. Eventually, the sounds of the storm seem to wind down.

"Do you think we can get up now?" I angle my head to look back at him.

"Probably." He loosens his arms so I can get out of the tub first. When I shift my weight, I feel something poke my back.

"Ew, Jake. Seriously?" I scramble up off him and gesture at his lap, where the evidence is obvious through his gym shorts.

He shrugs. "Sorry."

I narrow my eyes at him. I'm not convinced he feels apologetic at all.

"There's been a beautiful woman rubbing herself up against me for the better part of the afternoon, Lousy. Stuff is going to happen. What do you want me to do?"

His comment catches me off guard, and I pause for a second before responding. "Okay, A: Gross. And B: I absolutely wasn't rubbing myself against anything." Not intentionally, anyway. "And C: Did you hit your head? Do you realize you just called me beautiful? Me?" I can't remember the last time I received a compliment from Jake. Besides, no one calls me beautiful. Tiny, sure. Petite, yes. Occasionally someone's elderly aunty will say something that borders on positive about my features, like how my "angular face is quite striking." But beautiful? Never.

My stomach chooses this moment to grumble, loudly protesting the fact that it's almost dinnertime and all I've eaten today is one full cupcake and a half of another. I was serious when I said I don't want to consume too many of Danielle's wedding treats if we don't need to. The bridge could be fixed as soon as tomorrow for all we know, and I'm crossing my fingers that's the case. But in the meantime, I'm starving.

"I told you, you need to eat more of those cupcakes." Jake takes the opportunity to change the subject, and he gestures to my belly.

"I'm a grown-up, I decide what I eat. I do wish we had something a little more solid, though. You should tell your uncle to at least stock peanut butter in his rentals or something."

"Peanut butter is a liquid, but point taken."

"I don't think so," I argue. It's infuriating how I'm always second-guessing myself around Jake, but this is like basic third-grade science so I'm going to stand my ground. "It's a solid because it holds together and doesn't spread to take the shape of its container." If you put a blob of peanut butter on a slice of bread, it would stay put. Therefore, solid. Right? I'm almost positive I'm right about this.

"Oh, I'm going to love seeing your face when you Google this one. It's for sure a liquid. Try taking a jar of it on a plane and see what happens. Although, technically, it's a Bingham plastic like toothpaste, so I can see why you're confused."

"Oh my God, you are so patronizing and annoying."

He smirks and changes the subject again. "I think the rain let up for now. I'm going outside to assess the damage. I want to take some photos to send to Uncle Tim."

The sky has brightened. Although the forecast says the storms will continue on and off all day, more of the late afternoon sun is coming through the windows now, so he's probably right about the break in the rain. But I'd rather take a minute to discuss Jake calling me beautiful like it was no big deal.

He allowed that word to fly right out of his mouth as though it didn't shift the entire dynamic between us and alter my perception of reality in general, but now I can't bring it up again without looking like I'm fishing for compliments. Based on the things I've heard about my body for my entire life, I know for a fact what he said is not true. I'm not soft, or curvy, or round, or any of those other traditionally feminine adjectives. Still, it's flattering to hear, even if he was talking out of his ass.

But we have bigger priorities right now than discussing my bone structure. We need to figure out if we are likely to be stuck here with each other for the next few days. Together. Just me and the frenemy who only moments ago was sporting an impressive erection, apparently from proximity to *my* body. A body he just said he thinks is beautiful.

I shake my head and follow him to the yard. Thankfully, there doesn't seem to be much damage to his uncle's property other than what seems like hundreds of small fallen branches. None of them are big enough to cause any serious problems, but it will be quite a job to clean up. The creek has risen over the bank, but just barely. The water is still far enough away that it won't flood the house, at least as long as it doesn't start downpouring again. Jake starts scooping up sticks, so I follow his lead and do the same.

"You don't have to do that. You can go back inside." He straightens up to talk to me.

"It's fine. What else am I going to do? If I'm stuck here, I might as well make myself useful."

"Then wait a minute." He goes to the garage and digs until he finds a filthy pair of work gloves, then he returns and offers them to me.

"Ew. No. I'm not putting my hands in those. There could be spiders in them. Besides, they're too big for me and I don't know whose sweaty, hairy hands were in there last. I'll take my chances with the twigs."

"My hands, if you must know. These are mine. I wear them when I come out here to pull weeds." He shakes the gloves and looks inside each one, presumably to check for spiders, then he takes my wrist and places the gloves in my hand. "Put them on. Or don't. Do whatever you want. I don't care. But the last thing I need is to hear you whining about splinters for the next three days, and I'm not sure we have a decent first aid kit."

"If we're stuck together for that long, you won't have to worry about being around to hear anything. I will surely strangle you by the middle of Day Two," I say, accepting the gloves from him. They're gross and I don't want to wear them, but I don't want splinters either, so I compromise and only put one on my right hand, tucking the other one into the pocket of my cut-off jean shorts.

The two of us walk around the front yard gathering sticks and piling them in a heap. It reminds me of when we were young and we would play in the yard while Mr. Gibson raked.

"Do you remember when your dad would make those giant piles of leaves for us to jump in?"

He chuckles. "Yeah. I think my mom still has a few old photos of us with Danielle burying each other in those piles."

A beat of awkward silence passes, and I know we're both thinking the same thing. His parents tolerated me as a child, but I haven't been to the Gibsons' house in a long time. And, except for the wedding, I'm no longer welcome, especially after the incident last year.

I add another armful of twigs to the pile in front of us.

"That's probably good enough for now," Jake says. "Thanks for helping, Lousy."

"Could you not?" My voice cracks at the end of the question I didn't mean to ask. It slipped out because after the afternoon we've spent together, my guard is down.

"What?" He brushes the dirt from his clothes and stands still to look at me.

I clear my throat. It's hard not to squirm under his gaze. I hate that his nickname still has so much power over me. We're adults now. This shouldn't still hurt. I don't even think Jake's trying to be mean.

He's called Danielle 'Dan-Dan' for as long as I can remember, and although she says she hates it, we all know she doesn't. But that's a lot different than a nickname with head lice origins, and if I tell him it gets to me he's just as likely to double down as he is to stop.

"Don't worry about it. It's fine." I crouch down to pick up another stick. He tilts his head and furrows his eyebrows, studying me briefly before he gives up and walks back inside.

I make my way to the porch and take a few more minutes to myself.

When I go into the house, Jake is on the phone with his mom. I can only hear his side of the conversation, but based on the way he rubs his forehead and squeezes his eyes shut, my guess is it's going as well as I would expect it to go for someone to tell Shelia Gibson her precious baby is stuck overnight with the likes of me.

"We're fine, Mom. Jesus, no, do not call the National Guard… Sorry. No, you're right, I shouldn't swear at my mother…I do respect you…It doesn't really matter how we feel about her, I don't have a lot of options right now…can we just…Yes, I can appreciate your feelings…"

I thought maybe, after a year of fixating on it, I had blown that morning at their house out of proportion and my memory made it seem worse than it really was. But now I know it's not my imagination. His entire family hates me.

Chapter 9

Jake

This is exactly why I didn't want to make this call. My mom hardly lets me get a word in while she talks non-stop on the other end of the line.

"Why would you drive over the bridge when you knew there was a storm coming, Jacob? What were you thinking?"

I fight to keep my own voice steady while I try to calm her down. "I understand why you're worried, Mom. I really do. But I had no control over this situation."

That was the wrong thing to say because now she's back to lecturing me on all the things I should have done differently.

I cut her off. "Yes. Believe me, I know it's not ideal to be staying here, and maybe I should've asked Uncle Tim first. But it was an emergency, and I thought this might be preferable to drowning."

"Do you really believe this is the right time to be giving me lip?" She snaps at me and suddenly I'm five again. Somehow every conversation with my parents reduces me to a child.

I wince. "No, ma'am."

My mom starts in again without missing a beat. I put myself on mute and walk out to the garage, hoping Alice can't hear my mother lay into me. I dig through the car in search of anything useful while she drones on.

Thank God I'm moving out. I don't know Jordan well, but almost anything has to be better than dealing with this. Mom and I are getting nowhere. I'm not even sure why I called. I should've sent a proof of life text and blamed any lack of further communication on the weather. No matter what I do in this kind of situation, it will never be the right thing in my mother's eyes, and she's the easy one.

Score. There's a bag of jerky in the center console and an old granola bar in the glove compartment, along with the pack of baby wipes I use for Hazel's muddy paws when I take her to the park. I grab everything in one hand while I hold the phone to my ear with the other.

"Jacob, are you even listening?"

I have no idea what she said, but I unmute to tell her, "Alice and I are safe, and we can talk more about everything when I get home. Hopefully it won't be long, but we need to wait until they reopen the bridge. Can you please take care of Hazel for me? I'm glad she has you there. Love you, mom."

I hear her huff a disgruntled breath, but admitting I do still need her for something seems to appease her. For now.

I head back inside, where Alice is now sitting in the living room.

"I come bearing gifts." I toss the granola bar gently, and it lands next to her on the sofa.

"Thanks," she says, opening it and taking a bite while I tear into the jerky. She talks around a mouthful. "How long do you think it takes to develop scurvy?"

"Probably longer than a few days. Or else everyone who's ever spent a weekend living off cold pizza would be in trouble."

"Pizza at least has tomatoes on it, though. And sometimes peppers or pineapple."

I groan and sit next to her. "Please don't tell me you're a pineapple-on-pizza person."

She scoots further away and scrunches her face. "Say that three times fast. And yes, I am definitely a pineapple-on-pizza person. Didn't anyone ever tell you not to yuck someone else's yum?"

"Says the woman who is currently turning up her nose at my jerky."

"Because your jerky smells like someone dropped a leather shoe into a gallon of pepper and then sold it for consumption. In fact, you can't convince me that's not what's happening there." She points at my snack. "What did pineapple ever do to you? It's sweet, it's fresh, and it's real food."

"Pineapple by itself is fine. Pineapple on pizza is an abomination."

"Separatist."

"You know what? I'll make you a deal," I tell her. "You eat a piece of jerky, and when we get out of here, I'll buy us an entire pineapple pizza and I'll force myself to eat a slice." I actually do wish she'd eat the jerky. Maybe she'd be less inclined to bite my head off if she had a little more protein in her.

She seems to give my offer some serious consideration before responding. "I think we've reached a stalemate because, while I would like to put up a good fight for pineapples everywhere, I will not be putting your meat stick anywhere near my mouth."

I almost choke on the bite of jerky I'm chewing, but then I have to laugh.

Alice stomps off to the kitchen, I assume to get away from me. My eyes lock on those tiny denim shorts as she walks away. Every part of me except one knows it's a terrible idea, but if she ever changes her mind about wanting a taste of my meat stick, I'd happily oblige.

It's not long before she returns with a deck of cards in her hand. "Look what I found. Do you remember how to play Speed?"

I nod. At least now we have something to do to pass the time. I deal and Alice arranges her stack neatly in her hand while I divide the remaining cards into two piles on the table. It's been a long time since I've played Speed with anyone, but it comes back to me quickly. When I nod, we each turn over a card from one of the piles and begin stacking as fast as we can. She wins the first hand, but I win the second. By the third round, we are both hitting our stride as we flip our cards onto the piles. I have to admit, it's nice to hang out with her again. It reminds me of old times.

Alice must feel it too, because she raises her eyes to mine while she shuffles the deck and gives me a real smile, one I haven't seen in a long time. I miss seeing her look at me that way, and I still can't figure out exactly when everything shifted between us.

I stare at my cards because I'm too much of a coward to make eye contact when I say, "Can I ask you something? When did we stop being friends?"

Chapter 10

Alice

Does Jake really want to go there?

I swallow. I guess we're finally doing this.

"Did I do something specific to hurt you? Because if I did, that sucks and I'm sorry." He glances up from his cards.

I blink at him. Does he not remember what they did to me? He sits completely still waiting for me to speak. The only noise in the room is the scattered rhythm of rain hitting the roof again. The memories rush back in a tidal wave, and my heartbeat thuds in my ears.

"Allow me to jog your memory. It started around the time you joined the basketball team and began sitting with the guys at lunch. You and Danielle were still constantly hanging out together on weekends without me. She got to keep being treated like your best friend. But all of a sudden, I was just nothing."

Jake flinches and worry lines crease his forehead. "You were never nothing. I thought you were my friend, too. Then one day you just…weren't. And it didn't seem like you wanted to be. It felt like you started to hate me."

"I did. Well, that's too harsh. I didn't hate you, exactly, but I was hurt when you ditched me. Especially for your teammates."

"You were hurt because I made other friends?" He seems confused, but it feels like he is genuinely trying to understand.

It sounds so petty and stupid when he says it like that. Of course, our friendship didn't disappear overnight because he hung out with Danielle and his teammates more than he hung out with me. If that were all, I'm sure I'd be over it by now, but that was only the beginning.

"Jake, be real. It's not like my animosity came out of nowhere. Those new friends of yours almost ruined my life. And to this day you still call me 'head lice.' It doesn't exactly inspire warmth and tenderness. Let's not pretend this has been completely one-sided, okay?"

He seems to let my words sink in, and it takes a few seconds before he speaks again. "I'm going to need a lot more information about that first point before I can respond to it. But does it really bother you when I call you Lousy?" He can't be serious, and yet he is.

"Gee. Why would it bother someone if kids started calling her 'head lice' in middle school?"

He lets out a long breath. "Shit. That's a long time for you to carry that. I didn't mean anything by it. I thought you knew I was teasing. Although, I realize my intention is irrelevant if I actually did hurt your feelings. I'm sorry."

Dammit. Now I'm crying. I didn't realize how much I needed him to acknowledge that and apologize.

"Alice," he says softly, like he's testing the way my real name feels. "We don't have to talk about this anymore if you don't want to. I really am sorry."

My heart clenches and I nod at him. "Me, too. At least for the name-calling and stuff. I know I've done that to you, too." I wipe a tear away with my palm.

"You didn't do anything I didn't deserve," he assures me.

Yesterday I would have agreed with that statement. Now, I'm not so sure. It's funny how much can change in a day. Jake looks at me, and the sincerity in those deep brown eyes melts a layer of ice away from my heart.

I shake my head. "Forget it. We're good. Bygones or whatever. Let's get back to the game, yeah?"

Jake hesitates as if he wants to say something else, but then he nods, looks back down at his hand, and puts down a five. We continue in a steady rhythm until I slam my ace down on his king. I'm out of cards. I win.

"Okay, Ace. I see how it is." He chuckles. I lock eyes with him again, and we both smile. "Looks like we found you a new nickname," Jake says as he collects the cards to start a new round.

Chapter 11

Jake

We're both tired and ready to try to get some sleep, which is going to be hard to do with the wind still wailing outside. It's raining again, but with much less intensity. I wrestle the only mattress in the house over the railing, and it crashes to the floor below while Alice stands at the bottom of the steps, her hands on her hips.

"I still don't understand why we're doing this. Isn't it safer to sleep upstairs?" she calls up to me. "Higher ground and all that."

"If we expected to get ten feet of water in the house, that would make sense. But it's more likely we'll need to get to the car quickly if something happens, which is down here. And if there's another tornado tonight we should be as low to the ground as possible." Plus, there is safety in numbers. I know she won't share the bed. That's fine, I'll sleep on the sofa. But I don't want to leave her by herself on a separate floor of the house, and it's easier to move a mattress down a flight of stairs than it is to move a couch up.

"You take the bed. I can sleep on the couch," I tell her as I jog down the stairs and drag the mattress the rest of the way to the living room. I push the coffee table next to the couch to make space for it.

"No. That's dumb. You're like twice my size. It makes more sense for me to be the one to sleep on the sofa." She spreads out on the couch before I can argue.

"You know what? Fine. Just pick wherever you want, and I'll take the other option. How's that?" I'm not fighting with her about this. I know I won't be sleeping much anyway. I want to keep an eye on the weather.

Thunder cracks again and she practically jumps out of her skin. Then she clears her throat and smooths her shirt, pretending like nothing happened. But it's not hard to read her, especially with the way she won't stop chewing on her bottom lip. She's terrified, but I know if I say anything about her fear I'll only piss her off. The last thing she would want is to seem weak.

But when the next flash of lightning illuminates the entire room, Alice's wide eyes find mine.

"It's going to be fine," I tell her for what feels like the hundredth time. "The worst of it's over. We just need to figure out something to do to pass the time. Do you want to play cards again?"

She shakes her head, yawning.

As long as the weather doesn't take a turn, the worst part of being trapped here will be the boredom. I can handle a few days of cupcakes and Alice's attitude, but there's nothing productive we can do to occupy our time, and I'm already getting antsy.

We retreat to our designated sleep zones, and it isn't long before she's softly snoring on the couch, curled into a ball with her head on the armrest. I sit and stare, tracing the lines of her face with my eyes.

I still can't figure out what she meant about the other stuff that happened when we were in school, and I also can't believe I let her go years thinking I was trying to bully her with that stupid nickname. I would never try to hurt her on purpose. Not really. The insults and pranks just kind of evolved over time and became our thing. Besides, it's the only way she speaks to me these days, and I like how feisty she gets when we fight. I never meant to take it too far.

A tiny, contended sigh passes through her lips, and she smiles in her sleep. She looks so peaceful, but I don't want her to be cold, so I shake out a drop cloth and drape it over her. She shifts and inhales an adorable little snort, followed by a series of low, rumbling grunts. I chuckle to myself and take my phone off airplane mode just long enough to collect evidence.

Alice opens her eyes. "Do you always hover over sleeping women and film them without permission?" She sneers.

"I knew you wouldn't believe me otherwise. This proves how loud you were snoring. But don't worry. You're not even on camera."

I kept her face out of it on purpose. It's dark in the video, and I made sure to hold the phone so the shot is angled toward the ceiling.

She sits up and I take a seat on the couch to show her. She is not impressed.

"I do *not* snore. An eight-second video is hardly proof. And since I'm not in the frame, no one would know it was me. Full deniability."

"Oh, you most assuredly do." I laugh.

She folds her arms and taps one foot. "You're going to delete that video."

"As you wish, Princess Snores-a-Lot." I smirk and press the trash can icon on the bottom of the video, then I turn the screen so she can see it's been wiped from my phone.

"Delete it from the trash, too."

"Fine."

She watches while I clear it from my trash folder.

"Thank you." She swallows hard, and I bet she hopes I don't notice the way her voice waivers, but I do.

"Why are you so mad about this?" I try to soften my tone. I'm not sure why it's a big deal, but judging from her reaction, it definitely is. "I honestly didn't think it was that serious. Everybody snores sometimes. I thought you'd think it was funny, but you're right. I can see now it was out of pocket. My bad. I wasn't trying to embarrass you." Okay, maybe I was. Old habits die hard.

"I'm fine."

She won't look at me. She clearly isn't fine, and I can admit filming a woman while she was asleep was maybe not my brightest idea.

"Alice. Please look at me." I wait until those ice-blue eyes make their way up to mine before telling her, "I'm sorry."

"I said it's fine, Jake. Just drop it."

"I'm not going to drop it because I obviously upset you. If it makes you feel any better, I thought it was pretty cute."

She rolls her eyes. "You don't have to say that stuff to me."

"Why not? Are you tired of everyone telling you how pretty you are? I can get a little more creative if necessary."

She scoffs. "Jake, if we're really going to have this conversation, we should at least be honest with each other."

"I'm not following." I'm really not. I am being honest. It was freaking adorable.

She's wigging out about something that, in my eyes, seems pretty insignificant on the scale of the other pranks we've played. She's all over the place tonight, but one thing I know for sure is she's having an extra-hard time accepting a compliment. I know I'm not the only guy in this town who thinks Alice Caulfield is fine as hell. Most of them are just a little too scared to tell her that, for fear that she'll rip them a new one. It's a valid concern because she probably would, but that doesn't make her any less hot. If anything, it only adds fuel to the fire.

"You don't need to lie to me. I know how I look. I've seen mirrors. Nothing special is happening here." She points to herself. "So the flattery is falling pretty flat. No pun intended," she mumbles, looking down at her chest.

This isn't that thing some people do where they deny what you said, then encourage you to go on telling them more nice things about themselves. She really seems to believe this bullshit.

"Uh, were you looking in the distorted, fun house kind of mirrors? Because here in reality where the rest of us live, that sounds completely whack."

"Just…never mind. Can we drop it now?"

"Fat chance." It's beyond comprehension that Alice would say this stuff about herself. "Tell me why you think that."

"Because it's the truth? Like I said, I have eyeballs. And it's what people have been telling me my entire life." She sighs and sinks back into the couch.

"I'm going to need names." Who would tell her something like that?

Alice rolls her eyes again and hugs her arms around her stomach, but at least she's talking. We have nothing better to do tonight than get to the bottom of this, and I might have a few beefs to settle before this is over.

"I don't know. There are lots of examples. The girls in school, for one." She rubs the back of her neck.

"The Tinker Bell thing?" I always thought it was supposed to be a compliment when people called her that. As far as cartoon characters go, Tinker Bell is pretty sexy.

"Yes, there was that. Your mom has also made some comments. And my dad is always saying the reason I don't have a boyfriend is because nobody wants a woman with no curves. Women are supposed to be all tits and ass and I'm…not that."

"They actually said those words? That's really messed up. You know that, right?"

The soft light from the candles is casting shadows that flicker across her face. She sighs. "No, not those words exactly, but the sentiment was the same. I know they're not alone in those thoughts about me." Alice blinks quickly as tears pool in her eyes.

"The hell they aren't."

"That…is not my…experience." She fans her face with her hands and keeps blinking. It's not helping. She starts to sniffle despite her efforts.

My hand clenches at my side. Alice doesn't deserve this. I want to run out of here and beat the living hell out of everyone who made her feel this way about herself, but I stay still and quiet, trying to show her I'll listen when she's ready to talk.

One tear manages to fall, and finally, she whispers, "There was also that stuff that happened with your friends senior year."

"What stuff?" I try to dig through the recesses of my brain, but I honestly can't remember hearing any rumors about Alice.

Her eyes meet mine again. "Don't make me say it, Jake," she begs. "You know exactly what stuff."

"Louse—dammit. Sorry." My stomach drops. "Alice, I swear on Hazel's life, I have no idea what you're talking about."

She closes her eyes, inhaling a long breath. Then she lets it out slowly. "Do you remember when I went out with your friend Owen for a little while?"

"Vaguely."

Owen Myers was on the basketball team with me, but I wouldn't call him a friend. The guy was kind of a douchebag.

"Well, I did. I thought we really liked each other. After a month or so, when things started getting more serious, he asked for pictures." She pulls her legs up to her chest and wraps her arms around them, resting her chin on her knees. "I should have known better."

I don't like where this story is going at all.

"After a few more weeks, he was pressuring me to do more than I was ready to do, so I broke up with him. That's when he sent back screenshots of the photos. He said it was no big loss because he wasn't interested in flat, scrawny bodies like mine anyway. He told me hooking up with me would make him feel like a pervert because I was the size of a little girl."

"That's harsh."

"Yeah, that would have been bad enough on its own. But then he shared the pictures in a group text with his friends from the basketball team."

"What a dick!"

"And he sent me more screenshots. This time of all the nasty things they said, like every comment was new evidence proving him right."

"*What?*" I roar, flying to my feet. I pace in front of the couch, not knowing what else to do with the anger. I was the captain of that team and this shit was happening to my friend right under my nose?

She unfurls and covers her eyes with her hands. "I know. I should never have sent those kinds of shots. I don't know what I was thinking. My face wasn't in them. They were all from the neck down. But it wouldn't have been hard for the entire team to figure out who I was, even if Owen hadn't told them. I mean, I'm sure you saw them. Maybe it just wasn't very memorable." She looks down at her body again.

"I didn't see those pictures. And I sure as hell didn't know anything about any of this." We need to clear that up right now. I'm sure the team kept me out of the chat on purpose because there is no way I would have let that happen. Right now, I wish I had a time machine so I could go back to break every one of their phones and their noses.

She tilts her head, chewing her bottom lip again. This woman spent four years thinking I knew about this? Jesus. No wonder she started hating me. I'm surprised she still talks to me at all.

"You honestly thought I would do that to you?"

"Well, no. Not exactly," she admits. "None of the texts I saw were from you. It's just, those guys were your friends. So even if you weren't participating, you were hanging out with the people who did, and acting like it was no big deal."

"I swear I had no idea that was going on. This is the first I'm hearing about it. I'm so sorry that happened to you." I'm trying to take deep breaths and stay calm for her sake, but I want to put my fist through a wall.

I want to argue that if I had known I would've stopped it, but the disgusting truth is I don't know if that's true. I know there were times when I was younger when I was around guys doing inappropriate shit and I didn't speak up. Hell, I know I did some of it, too. Nothing of this magnitude, but still. It does not feel good to have to admit to myself. The back of my neck burns with the memory of all the stupid things I said about girls. But never about my own friends. Never about Alice.

"Listen, I don't care what kind of pictures you sent him. There is absolutely nothing you could have done to deserve that. It doesn't even sound legal."

"It's not. I looked it up." She sighs and her shoulders slump. "I even called a lawyer for a free consultation, but they said it's only a misdemeanor in Virginia. Even if I had the money or the energy to fight him, which I don't, taking it to court would mean having to share the photos with law enforcement and lawyers."

She blows out a long breath as she pulls her legs back up to her chest. "I was eighteen, so I was a legal adult when I sent them, and I gave them to him on purpose. The whole thing would drag on for months, or maybe even years. And even then, the maximum fine they could give him for distributing revenge porn is still less than I would have to pay my lawyer. Besides, we're past the statute of limitations now. I need to put it behind me. But it's hard."

Of course it's hard. God, she looks so defeated. I don't know where Owen is now, but if I ever find out, he's going to pay. But I don't think that's what she wants to hear.

I sit next to her. "Owen Myers once ate an entire unlit cigarette because someone offered him a dollar. He's a moron and a dickhead. I wouldn't trust his judgment about anything. Definitely not your body."

"Is that supposed to make me feel better?" she mumbles into her knees.

"Hey. Look at me." I move close to her and use my index finger to lift her chin. "Have I ever been the kind of guy to blow smoke up your ass?"

She laughs, despite the tears falling from the corners of her eyes. "No. You never hold back just to spare my feelings. It's one of your more annoying qualities."

Ouch, but fair. I need to work on that.

"Okay. That's how you know I'm telling you the truth. I don't lie to you. I mean, I guess I did deny putting the tuna in your car. That was me. But I never lie to you about important stuff. So, yeah. When I tell you that I think you're hot, it means I think you're hot. I don't give two flying shits what any other assholes said."

She wipes her nose on the back of her hand and rolls her eyes again, but this time she offers a weak smile. "Behold the beautiful words every little girl grows up wanting to hear. Look, you don't have to try to comfort me, Jake. To be honest, you kind of suck at it. Besides, you've never even liked me."

I hate how long I let her believe that.

"That's not true. Dammit, Alice. Of course I like you."

"Right. Sure you do." The sarcasm in her voice is heavy as she nods.

"Sometimes you drive me out of my mind, but it never meant I didn't like you. I like tons of stuff about you."

"You're so full of it."

"Fine. You want honest? I like that I never know what color your hair is going to be the next time I see you. I like the way you smell like fruit, and I like how you always call me on my own shit. And yes, I also think you're hot, okay?" My voice lowers to almost a whisper as I tell her, "But right now, when you're sitting there staring at me with those big blue eyes, you make me want to make the whole world softer so you can't get hurt like this again. I wish I could make everyone else understand that, yeah, you're strong as hell, but you also need a safe place to land when you go flying off the handle. Which is, like, all the time, by the way. And I... I kind of like the idea that today I could be the one to do that for you."

She turns her head to face me and rests her cheek on her knees for a second before shifting to tuck her legs under her body. "Really?"

"Yes, really."

"Tell me something else," she whispers. "Something true."

I don't even have to think about it. "The way you're looking at me right now makes me want to kiss you."

"Jake." Her voice is soft and her skin is flushed from crying.

"Yeah?" I cringe and brace for the rejection I know is coming. Maybe I went a little too far with that last one. She's vulnerable right now, and I don't want her to think I'm trying to take advantage.

"I think I want that, too."

She doesn't have to tell me twice. I lean toward her and wrap one hand around the back of her head. She nods her confirmation just before our mouths meet. It starts slow and soft because I don't want to rush her, but when she fists her hand in my shirt and takes control, I'm not about to stop her. When she opens her mouth, I can taste the sweetness from the cupcake icing lingering on her tongue. I move closer and pull her body to mine.

Chapter 12

Alice

The hurricane must have opened a portal to an alternate universe. It's the only logical explanation. The entire world has turned upside down in one afternoon because I'm sitting on a dust-covered couch in an abandoned house, and I'm kissing Jake. *Really* kissing him. My tongue is in his mouth right now. Because I put it there. On purpose.

I let go of him and pull away. We're both breathing heavily, and his pupils are wider than they were before. What are we doing?

"Sorry," I tell him, sliding back to my own cushion. I brush my fingers over my swollen lips. "I don't know what I was thinking."

"Oh, you're sorry, huh?" He smirks playfully.

"Yeah. I am."

"Okay. Then I'm sorry, too. But only because I didn't make you feel like you could tell me about Owen sooner. I'm not sorry about the rest of this at all." He gestures between our bodies. There's still a small smile playing with the corner of his lips.

His other arm is slung over the back of the sofa, and he twirls a strand of my hair with his fingers. That tiny motion doesn't have any right to be as hot as it is, but feeling his fingers brush my neck gives me goose bumps.

I roll my eyes for probably the millionth time today, but there's no longer any fight behind it, and he pulls a smile out of me before he leans in to kiss me again. And I let him. After the next soft brush of his lips against mine, my reservations dissolve and I fully give in. My mouth crashes into his with a reckless urgency that has our teeth and tongues fighting for space. I move my hands to his neck and link my fingers together at the base of his head.

"We shouldn't," I murmur.

"Maybe not," he whispers in my ear before gently nipping my lobe. "But I really, really want to."

He bucks his hips into mine as he tugs my lower lip between his teeth.

"We really, really shouldn't," I mumble between hurried, ungraceful kisses.

His breath deepens, but he plants his hands on my hips, as if he's waiting for me to make the next move. "We can stop. Or not. Whatever happens next is up to you."

I groan and pull him back to me. I don't want to stop. I grab at the hem of his hoodie, and he leans back to take it off while I trace his abs with my fingers. His patience is walking the line between infuriating and endearing because I already feel like my body is on fire, and I don't know how he has so much self-control. I kiss him again. My own desperate need to feel wanted fogs up my brain while his tongue explores mine

Years of tension, frustration, and unspoken attraction pass between us, and even though it's chilly in this dark, drafty house, there's a new warmth spreading through me. The waves of heat and intense emotion are almost too much. I know how dangerous this is for our delicate friendship, but it's also too exhilarating to make myself stop.

I break the kiss to tell him, "Whatever happens tonight, it doesn't leave this room."

"If that's what you want," he agrees without missing a beat.

"I'm not really sure what I want," I admit.

"That's okay. Come here." Jake pulls me onto his lap with one arm hooked around my waist, so my back is pressed to his chest. "We'll figure it out together." His warm breath raises the hairs on my neck, and I can feel the thud of his heartbeat when he holds me closer to him like we're in the bathtub again. "Is this what you want?"

He runs his nose along the skin behind my ear. I arch into him and turn so my face meets his. Reaching up with one hand, I tug him back into a quick kiss before tapping the arm that is pinning me in place. He loosens his grip so I can shift my body, and I turn to straddle him, my knees sinking into the couch cushions on either side. I grind on him while my fingers roam through his hair, lightly scratching his scalp. He closes his eyes and leans back into the sofa, and I drag my nails down his chest.

"Is this what *you* want?" I volley the question back to him.

He chuckles darkly and puts his hands on my hips again, pressing me down into his lap. "I think we can both feel the answer to that. But I'm not doing anything until you ask for it."

"That's too bad. Guess we're going to be here for a while, then." I tease as I rub against him.

"You won't hear me complaining."

He looks into my eyes and I feel almost drunk on his attention. His strong hands guide my hips in fluid circles as I ride his lap, fully-clothed like some horny coed. Low sounds rumble in his throat, and his Adam's apple bobs. I feel a rush of power as his body reacts to mine. I run my thumb down his neck while he swallows, and I can't explain why that's the thing that snaps my last thread of control.

"Kiss me." I lean forward.

Jake moves a hand to my face. "I'm pretty sure that's what we're already doing." He holds me still while he plants searing kisses from the corner of my mouth, down my jaw, until he reaches the sensitive spot at the base of my neck, sending chills through my entire body. "Is there somewhere else you want me to kiss you?" he asks, guiding my body to lie down on the sofa. "Like here?" He moves lower and kisses my collar bone. "Or maybe here?" His voice is a raspy whisper as he moves to the other side, this time slowly working his way up from my neck to my earlobe. I groan as his fingers toy with the waistband on my shorts and he shifts us so he can fit next to me. "Where Alice?"

Hearing my name in his smooth bedroom voice makes me whimper. I know I might regret this in the morning, but I don't care, because I also know if I stop now I'll regret it even more.

So, I reach down and slide out of my shorts. Jake gives me a hungry smile as he reaches for his wallet on the coffee table and produces a condom.

"This just gives us options," he says calmly, laying the condom on the table next to the open box of cupcakes. "We don't have to go that far. We can stop right now and go back to playing cards if that's what you want." He offers me an out, but I shake my head because I'm not taking it.

"Come here," I tell him. "I want you."

"Good." He kisses me again and drops to his knees on the mattress on the floor. "Because I've wanted you like this since the morning you walked out of my bedroom wearing my shirt." He takes my hands and pulls me down on top of him.

I moan while our bodies glide together. I don't know if I should tell him I still sleep in that shirt almost every night.

Chapter 13

Jake

The way her nails are digging into my shoulders while her lower half grinds against me tells me she wants this as much as I do. Her thighs clench my sides as my fingers tease and slide around her body.

"I like that." She hums.

"I can see that. Me, too." But the last thing I want is for her to wake up tomorrow with regrets. "You're sure about this, right, Ace?" I ask, slowing my fingers to a gentle caress.

She props herself up on her elbows and lets out a frustrated groan. "For God's sake. Take a hint, Jake. It's a yes. Do you need it in writing or something?"

"Oh, there she is." I smile down at her, glad to see her fiery side again. "I was wondering if Sassy Alice was coming back out to play tonight."

She sighs, but I can tell she's holding back a smile of her own. "Don't worry. She never left."

"Good. I like Sassy Alice."

I see the question in her eyes before she voices it. "Really?"

I nod at her. "Don't get me wrong. I'm also really enjoying getting to know Likes-Fooling-Around-in-Abandoned-Houses Alice, but Sassy Alice has always been my favorite."

She laughs, and the sound makes my whole body feel lighter. "Ok, now *I'm* going to need *that* in writing, so I can frequently remind you of the time you admitted you like it when I'm snarky with you."

I shrug. "Guilty."

Leaning over Alice's body, I grab a cupcake from the coffee table. I pinch off some cake from the bottom and bring it to her lips. She opens, and I alternate feeding her bites of cake and brushing the crumbs away with kisses until all we have left is the blue icing in my hand.

I use my free hand to tuck the fabric of her shirt up into her bra and expose her stomach.

"What are you doing?" She eyes the icing, curious.

"Improvising. You said you need to see it in writing. I aim to please. While we're at it, we're going to replace all those ugly words you said about yourself with new ones. I want you to see what I see." I dip my index finger into the icing and use it to paint the word "sexy" on her belly. "Tell me what that says."

She rolls her eyes, but I raise my eyebrows and wait until she finally says it.

"Good job," I praise her, and she smiles. Then I trace over the word with my tongue, licking my canvas clean.

I don't want them all to be physical, so I follow up with words like *strong*, *fun*, and *feisty*, making her read each word out loud before I lick it off. But because this *is* physical, I move on to marking all the parts of her I find attractive. Using my thumb, I smear a dot on her nose. "This is adorable," I say, leaning in to kiss the icing away.

Her breath is heavy as she watches me.

"And looking at this makes me want to suck on it." I add another dollop of icing to her collar bone and do exactly that. "These are cute, too." I smear small blue streaks onto each of her earlobes before I kiss them away.

She giggles. Then she pulls her shirt over her head, and I'm transfixed as I watch her slowly peel off her bra.

The candlelight flickers and shadows pass over her smooth, pale skin. I'm not sure if I've ever called someone breathtaking, but there is no other word, because seeing her naked body in front of me steals all the air right out of my lungs.

Alice laughs as she swipes a smear of blue from her forearm with her finger. "What if I want to paint, too?" she asks as she brings the icing to my lips.

I suck it away. "You're more than welcome." I put out my arms and offer my chest as her canvas.

She peers up at me from under her lashes, then she trails her wet finger down my stomach to the top of my shorts. "Take those off for me?"

"Are you sure?"

She nods and whispers a very definitive, "Yes."

I slide them off, along with my boxer briefs, and toss my clothes to the side of the mattress. I can't help but smirk when her eyes widen. She uses two fingers to scrape some icing from my palm. It's cold and sticky as she smears it on, and complete ecstasy as her warm mouth licks and sucks all of it away.

"I'm ready, Jake. I want you." The best six words in the English language.

"Great. Little help?" I hold up my icing-covered hands and nod at the condom because she is going to have to be the one to put it on. She laughs and grabs it from the table, using her teeth to help her tear into the foil before she rolls it onto me.

Nothing has ever felt as good as Alice does when I sink into her.

"Jake." She inhales a shaky gasp.

I lied. Hearing the need in her voice when she whispers my name is even better.

Time means nothing anymore. There is only her, and me, and this moment. I ignore the ache in my forearms as I drown in those eyes. She brings both hands to my face and pulls me down into another kiss. I can tell she's almost there when she starts moving faster and her breathing changes.

"I…I need…oh…I'm going to…"

I lower myself to her ear.

"I know. I know what you need." Those are the words that push her over the edge, and I feel her pulse and squeeze around me.

"Jake," she says my name again, and a primal groan rips from the depths of my soul as I fall right behind her.

Chapter 14

Alice

I can now confirm that Jake Gibson is *very* good with his hands. And his mouth. And other things. I'm a little tired and sweaty, but in the best way, like after a great Pilates workout. Best of all, the noise in my head is quiet for the first time in ages. Jake lies next to me with both hands behind his head, and I snuggle into the crook of his arm. The drop cloth, now stained with streaks of blue food coloring, has become our makeshift blanket for the evening. I hardly notice the scratchy fabric as I run my fingers over his tattoos.

At first, the ink on his right arm seems to be an intricate landscape, but looking closer I can see it's Hogwarts. The Castle is there, although it's not the main focus. The animals done in white ink seem to be flying. It's like a hidden picture book, trying to spot them all.

"I've never seen your tattoo up close. It's pretty sweet," I tell him, tracing the pictures on his arm.

"It's from Harry Potter."

"I know. I like the way you added the Patronuses. Patroni? What's the plural of Patronus?"

He chuckles. "Couldn't tell you. The white ink is going to fade pretty quickly, but I kind of like it that way because that's how a Patronus works in the story. It's not there forever."

"True. What's this one?" I motion to his left arm.

"The Battle of Isengard from *The Lord of the Rings*. The one where the Ents fight. Do you remember Treebeard, the old talking tree?"

Can't say that I do.

"Oh, I see. So, you're like a real nerd's nerd?" I tease.

"Says the lady who knows about Patronuses. I guess I just like the idea of good and evil or right and wrong being so black and white. Things are more complicated in real life."

Don't I know it. "Fair. What's your Patronus?"

"I want to say something cool like a lion or a fox, but in reality, it's probably a beaver or something."

"Ah, nature's engineer."

Jake chuckles. "How about you?"

"I don't know, honestly."

He looks up at the ceiling. "Maybe a lightning bug?" After a beat, he nods. "Yeah, I think that's it."

"Why, because I'm such a pest?" I smile.

"Nah, I wouldn't say they're pests. No one's calling an exterminator for lightning bugs. They're the one bug people actually look forward to seeing. When I was a kid, chasing lightning bugs was one of my favorite parts of the summer. Tiny, bright, ethereal. Sounds like someone else I know." He looks down at me and my stupid heart flutters as if it doesn't know better.

"That might be the nicest thing you've ever said to me, Gibson."

"Don't get used to it," he teases.

"Don't worry, I won't. I know this is a one-time thing."

I need to remind myself this bubble is temporary. When we get home everything will go right back to the way it was.

"It can be. If that's what you want."

The way he phrases that sentence sets my teeth on edge. It sounds like a cop-out on his part, like he's absolving himself of all responsibility and putting all the decisions on me. If that's the way he wants to play it, fine.

"We both know what this is, Jake."

"Do we?"

"Yes. One night of great sex. One. Night."

"Of great sex." He chuckles again while he repeats my own words back to me. "Can I get *that* in writing? You planning to leave a five-star review?"

"Sure. And I guess I should send out a few dozen thank you cards to your exes while I'm writing things. Turns out all of that practice was a good thing after all."

Okay, that might have crossed a line.

"Excuse me?" He cocks a brow at me.

I definitely crossed a line.

The logical voice in my head is screaming at me to stop, but the fighter who needs to protect my heart is doing all the talking. She wants to stop this before I go and do something stupid. Like fall for Jake Gibson.

"Oh, come on, Jake. Who do you think had to talk Danielle off the ledge every time you were parading through The Blue Crab with some skanky townie? Or getting tagged in a photo with a random sorority girl hanging all over you?" Ew. This isn't me. I don't call other women skanky.

"Right. Okay. So, you think having a meal or being in a picture with someone automatically means I slept with them?" He shakes his head and turns to grab his clothes from the floor. Then he stands to pull his shorts over his hips.

"I said it was good. It's a compliment."

"Is it? Actually, you said it was *great*. So break out the thank you cards. And I'll write some to the scores of men you must've been with to make what we did that great."

"Hey. That's not fair. Don't slut shame me."

He raises his eyebrows and crosses his arms over his bare chest, waiting for me to acknowledge the double standard in what I just said. He's going to be waiting for a long time because I'm not going to do it, and also a big part of me would be perfectly content to sit here all night and stare up at those pecs.

Instead I offer, "You wouldn't have many cards to write. I've only ever gone that far with two people. And one of them is you."

"I'm not having this conversation." He turns and walks toward the bathroom.

He's not getting away from me that easily. I wrap myself in the makeshift drop cloth blanket and follow him down the dark hall. Once I'm standing in the doorway, I realize I don't have a plan. I stand there watching him, my whole body tense and ready to fight. His cell phone sits on the small counter giving off a blue glow that lights the room.

He scrubs a hand down his face and mumbles something that sounds like *fine, have it your way* before he turns to the toilet and drops trou while simultaneously tossing the condom in the trash.

"Ew, what are you doing?" I turn to face away from him and cover my ears with my hands to block out the splash while he pees.

"What am *I* doing? What does it look like?"

"Well, stop."

He huffs out a sardonic laugh. "I'm not the one following people into the bathroom. I'm not sure what you thought was going to happen, but this is what people do in here." I uncover my ears, because it wasn't helping anyway, as he flushes and refills the toilet tank with the bucket of rainwater he brought in earlier. Then he tries to turn on the faucet to wash his hands, but nothing comes out. He grunts, and I hear him pull a baby wipe from the package he left sitting by the sink.

I spin back around as he calmly wipes his hands, eying me in the mirror. Even though I can't see my reflection, it strikes me how ridiculous I must look. I don't know what kind of hurricane-force idiocy brought us to this moment. I can't keep a lid on my emotions around Jake under normal circumstances, but after everything that's happened tonight, the cocktail of nerves and lust has turned me into a version of myself I don't recognize.

He turns to face me.

"Never mind. I don't even care," I say, trying to save a small shred of my dignity.

"Obviously, you do." He leans back onto the counter, arms crossed again. "Why do you care, Alice?"

My voice is a tiny whisper when I tell him, "I don't know. I just do." I look at the dingy tile floor because I can't make eye contact.

He sighs. "What do you want to know?"

"Wait, really?"

I look back up at him, feeling even more naked than before.

"You shared some really personal stuff with me earlier, so I guess this is fair. You get three questions. I'm only giving one-word answers. Then we're dropping this for good. Go."

I swallow. "How many others?"

"Five."

"Do I know them?"

"Maybe." He shrugs.

"Who? Wait, no. I don't actually think I want to know. I shouldn't have asked. It wasn't cool of me. Sorry. That's not my last question."

He smirks with an irritating patience and shrugs again as I ramble. He's still not wearing a shirt, and his muscles are distracting, making me fumble through my thoughts. I only have one question left. I might as well ask the thing I really want to know.

"How do you feel about me right now?" I try to stand up straight. I refuse to be embarrassed for having emotions or being human. But why is it so much harder to ask this question than it was to literally invite him inside of me?

He uncrosses his arms and rubs his jaw. I force myself to hold his stare, willing my body not to hunch over in defeat while he takes his sweet time finding an answer.

Finally, he scratches his chin and settles on, "Favorably."

"Favorably?" I repeat, slowly.

On one hand, I should hope he feels *favorably*. He spent an inordinate amount of time tonight face-to-face with places of my body that not even I have seen up close and personal. It would be a real dick move to say anything negative after all of that. On the other hand, I did follow him into this bathroom to interrogate him like a psychopath, so who could blame him if he has a different answer now?

He smirks again. "That's the best I can do with one word."

I guess I'll take favorably.

I scoot to the side, making space for him to walk out of the room. Instead, he closes the space between us with two easy strides and rests his hands on the wall on either side of me, caging me in. He's so much taller than I am, and his body completely eclipses mine while he makes a show of looking up and down my body.

"I'm sorry," I whisper at the floor. "I don't know why I'm acting this way."

"Look, the turn things took tonight came as a surprise to me too, Ace. But I have no regrets. And if tonight is all we're getting, I recommend you lose the sheet because we are far from finished."

I channel every ounce of confidence I can to look up into his eyes. "Is that so?"

Jake holds my gaze as I let the icing-stained fabric fall from my hands and pool around my feet. Then I duck under his arm, and I feel his eyes on me as I walk down the hall wearing nothing at all.

Chapter 15

Alice

Wednesday morning is a blur. We spend it in bed, eating more cupcakes and inventing creative ways to burn them off. When we've both had our fill of the cupcakes and each other, we lie in a tangled mess of limbs and fabric. Jake's hand trails lazily down my back, but then it slows and stills.

"Can I ask you something?"

I'm not used to hearing him sound nervous. It's kind of adorable. "Sure."

"You know how I told you all that stuff I like about you?"

As if I will ever forget. I nod to encourage him to go on.

"Well, is there anything…you know, never mind. It's dumb." He almost sounds shy.

"Aw. Are you trying to ask me what I like about you, Gibson?"

"I mean, if I had to say all that stuff out loud, it only seems fair."

I laugh. Then I close my eyes and take a breath before I speak again, because after all the time we spent fighting and trying to push down our feelings for each other, it still feels strange to give them a voice. "Fine. You're funny." I pause and run a finger over his abs, making him wait before I go on. "You're creative, you're fun to be around, and you're really loyal to the people you love. You make me feel safe. It's easy to let go and lose control around you because I know you can handle every version of me. And you're not half-bad to look at. Happy?"

"Very."

"Any more questions?"

He moves his head from side to side as if he's weighing whether he should say what else is on his mind. When he does, I wish I hadn't asked. "Just the big one. What happens when the bridge opens? Is the plan still not to tell anyone about this?"

My heart clenches. "Jake. You know we can't. Your mom practically had a coronary at the idea of you being stuck here with me. Plus, Danielle and Mike are getting married this weekend. We can't pull the focus away from their big day with news about us. Especially when there isn't even an 'us.'"

He nods, but he doesn't look at me. "Yeah. That's what I figured."

I snuggle closer into him. "We don't have to think about it yet. We're still here. And I, for one, plan to enjoy the break from real life now that we're no longer in mortal danger. No school. No work. No family drama. We can sleep as much as we want. Or do…other stuff." I wiggle my eyebrows. "If we only had some actual food, this would be a perfect day."

Jake kisses my forehead and gestures at the room. "Technically, I am at work right now."

"Don't worry, I know the property manager. I'm sure he's okay with it."

He chuckles as his hand finds mine. "Oh, he definitely is. Tell me about your job. Danielle said you're writing now?"

I shift my body and look at the ceiling. "Yeah. It's going okay, I guess. I've made a decent number of sales. But I'm taking a writing class with a professor who doesn't like my work at all, and it's messing with my head a little."

He squeezes my hand. "I'm sure your stuff is great."

I shrug and nuzzle into his chest. "Your turn. Tell me something I don't know about you."

"I think I want to open an art studio," he tells the top of my head.

"Really? Wow. That's big."

"Yeah, well. My dad's been on my case about not having a real job, but I can't see myself spending the next forty years in corporate America wearing a tie and saying things like, 'Let's circle back to where we dropped the ball in quarter two.'"

I can't picture that for Jake either. It would make him miserable.

"I was thinking a community studio would be cool. I could show other artists' work. Or just have a creative space to host classes or something. If I can find a building. In the meantime, I'm going to teach some free art classes at the library."

"Really? That sounds awesome."

"Your turn to tell me something."

"I miss real food. I had a dream about pizza last night."

He laughs and squeezes me tighter. "And here I thought all that moaning you were doing might have something to do with me."

"Nope. Sorry. It was the pizza."

We chat about nothing and everything until I drift off to sleep in Jake's arms.

In the morning, I wake up to find him sitting at the foot of the mattress, looking at his phone. He turns to me, the expression on his face unreadable.

"My mom called. The bridge is open."

"Oh. Um, wow. Then back to reality, I guess?"

After a beat, he nods.

We're quiet as we haul the mattress back up the stairs and into the bedroom. Then we clean ourselves up with some of the baby wipes and gather the rest of our things. As we leave the house, Jake stands at the garage entrance with his hand on the doorknob. He hesitates briefly, but then he opens the door for me, and we climb into the car.

He's the first one to speak. "Is it weird to say I don't know if I'm ready to go back yet?"

"Maybe, but I know what you mean." I give him a soft smile. "Pizza?"

My stomach rumbles on cue. "Yes, please! But then home so I can finally brush my teeth with actual toothpaste."

He drives to an Italian restaurant in Marnock. After living on cupcakes, the smell of savory garlic and tomato perfection that hits my nose when we walk in might be actual nirvana. The sign by the door says to seat ourselves, so I find a table and plop myself down. I expect Jake to sit across from me, but he takes the chair next to mine. We each order a medium pizza for ourselves and dig in as soon as they arrive. I even convince Jake to try a bite of my cheese-free slice loaded with veggies and pineapple. He won't admit it's good, but he doesn't spit it out either, so I'm calling it a win.

"Will you judge me if I order another pizza?" I ask as I start my fourth slice. After three days without a solid meal, I'm famished.

"Only if that one also has pineapple on it."

I laugh through another bite.

"Are you missing any classes today?" he asks.

"Nah. When they saw how bad the storms were, they canceled for the rest of the week." I chew slowly, curious about his own education. Once I swallow, I say, "Can you clear something up for me? How does Jacob Gibson fail out of school? Aren't you supposed to be some kind of genius?"

"Of all people, you should know better than to believe that." He chuckles, but then he shifts in his chair.

"Jake." I pin him with a look. "Come on. I know something happened."

"Nothing happened. Drop it, Alice."

My name sounds cold and distant coming from him now, like he's building back up the wall that was between us for years. I don't want to let that happen again.

"What did you say to me when I told you to drop your probing questions about how I felt about my body? *Fat chance*? We're supposed to be friends now. Tell me what happened."

He groans. "I knew that one would come back to bite me."

"Give me something true," I say, still trying to hold onto our time at the cottage.

"Look, I don't have some salacious, juicy story for you. It feels dumb to even talk about it. But the whole college scene just wasn't for me. The school was fine, the people were fine. But the pressure to continue to be someone I'm not was too much. I felt like if I didn't get out, I was going to self-destruct. It was just…really bad for my mental health. End of story. Leave it alone." His bossy tone is back.

"Yes, daddy," I mock. I roll my eyes at him, which is just automatic at this point. As much fun as we've had over the past couple of days, he's still ridiculous and exhausting.

His gaze snaps back to my face, and I swear he bores a hole right through my center of gravity with those deep brown eyes. "You're playing with fire talking to me like that, baby girl."

Well, damn. R.I.P. my self-respect because I'm pretty sure my nether regions have spontaneously incinerated. The way he's looking at me makes me want to do something insane, like climb over there and jump him in public. But I'm not going to do it, obviously. We agreed we are never doing that again. Plus, I'm like ninety percent sure he would reject me and then never let me hear the end of it. Although, the way he's still looking at me makes me think maybe that number is lower. Seventy-five percent chance of rejection?

He tightens his jaw, eyes still locked on mine. Fifty percent chance? I can't believe I'm actually considering if it might be worth the risk. When he subtly licks his bottom lip my shudder is involuntary. He smirks. He knows exactly what he's doing. God, I hate his stupid face, but I also can't stop looking at it. He knows it, too.

This might be the worst thing about living in a small town. There's no such thing as a casual no-strings-attached hookup. Jake

Gibson in particular comes with *all* of the strings, and it's just not worth it. No matter how much my body is protesting this decision.

I swallow, resisting all my other urges. "Just so you know, there's no shame in quitting something that isn't working for you. And there's definitely no shame in wanting to take care of your mental health."

The heat in his eyes fades away. "Thanks, but try being the one to tell Ward and Shelia Gibson their only son is a drop-out."

"Yeah, I can imagine that didn't go over very well."

"You can say that again."

"That sucks. I'm sorry."

"It's all good. I'm figuring things out." He gathers our scrunched-up napkins off the table. "Come on, you ready?"

I nod and follow him back to the car.

Once we're over the bridge, I turn to him. "Seriously, Jake. That was a lot of fun. But we can't do it anymore, and we can't tell anyone what happened this weekend." That little panty-melting glitch at the restaurant was confusing.

"I heard you the first twenty times. The message has been received. I already told you, I'm not going to say anything. I'm not in the habit of discussing my sex life with anyone. Besides maybe when someone gets a little needy." He widens his eyes at me, mocking.

I probably deserve that.

When we pull up to my house, Jake puts a hand on my shoulder. "Goodbye, Ace." He squeezes lightly, just once.

My skin still tingles from his touch as he drives away.

Inside, my dad is holding a beer and grumbling at the TV. When he sees me, he lowers the aluminum can in his hand.

"Where the hell have you been?" Dad directs his grumbles toward me.

"Didn't you get my message? We were doing some errands for the wedding and got trapped in Marnock because the bridge was out."

"That's a damn lie. Your little friend came by yesterday to ask if I needed anything."

"I never said Danielle was there. We were doing her a favor and picking up the cupcakes from the bakery when the storm rolled in."

"*We.*" He takes a slow sip. "Funny how you never mentioned who that meant. That fancy car you just climbed out of belongs to the Gibsons' boy."

I don't say anything.

"You've been shacked up with him all week, leaving me here to do everything alone," he scoffs.

My eyes flash to the dirty paper plates at his feet and the used tissues on the tray next to him. The rest of the house looks the same as it did when I left on Tuesday.

He grunts. "Should have known. You always did take after your mother. She was a pretty thing, and damn that woman could cook, but she couldn't keep her legs closed either. That's what started all of this."

I flinch at his accusation, and he crumples the now-empty can and tosses it to the floor with the discarded plates. I know better than to engage with my dad when he's like this.

I close my eyes and try to imagine his words rolling off my back like water droplets. But it doesn't work. Because, unlike what happened with Shelia and Ward, this time his assumption I slept with Jake is true.

This is exactly why I didn't want anyone to know, and why we can never let it happen again.

Chapter 16

Jake

The wedding party has taken over my parents' house. Mike, Jordan, and I are in my childhood bedroom, which is looking sparse since I've relocated most of my things to the apartment. There are paint swatches on the wall. It's a little depressing how quickly my mom started redecorating. I've only seen Alice briefly today because she's busy helping Danielle. Today is the first time we've been in the same space since I took her home after the storm.

The guys are standing around making uncomfortable small talk, waiting until we get word that the ladies are ready. We're all wearing matching tan suits, and our ties are the same shade of Carolina blue as Alice's bridesmaid dress.

"Hey man, could you give these to Danielle for me before we get started? She'll understand." Mike says, handing me a pack of peanut M&M's.

I nod, grateful for the opportunity to have something to do, and I cross the hall to knock on the door of my parents' bedroom where Danielle and her girls are getting ready. I try not to read too much into the wave of nerves that hits me, knowing Alice is on the other side.

"Is everybody decent in there?" I call out. The last thing I want is to walk in on any of the Daniels women changing, but it wouldn't be the worst thing in the world if I happened to catch a glimpse of the maid of honor.

"We're all dressed if that's what you mean, but you'll never hear me promise to be decent," Ms. Honey yells from the other side of the door. I laugh as I open it, but as soon as I see my best friend standing there in her wedding gown, all the air is knocked out of me.

"Danielle." It comes out in a whisper so tender I hardly recognize my own voice.

"It's just a dress. Still me in here under all of this fabric. Call me Dan-Dan. It will make this all feel more normal."

"I can do that." I nod at her and clear my throat. "Mike asked me to give you these?" I take the M&M's out of my pocket.

Honey lets out a loud laugh from the chair where she sits in the corner. "Always with the candy, that one."

"I'll just set them down here," I say, putting the candy on a chair next to Danielle's purse.

"Are you ready?" Ms. Heather asks, smoothing the back of her daughter's dress.

"As much as I'll ever be."

I scoot out of the way and let the women walk ahead of me. Alice hangs back, too. She stops next to me to put on her heels, using my elbow to balance as she slips on a shoe and adjusts the strap.

"Hey, stranger. Rough day?" she asks, pinning me with a knowing look.

I shrug one shoulder, not wanting to admit it, but somehow it's become impossible for me to lie to her. "Maybe just a little. Better now that I get to see you in this dress. Damn."

She smiles and her eyelids flutter. "Nuh-uh. No flirting. We don't do that anymore."

"In my defense, it's true." I want to tell her exactly how good she looks with her hair curled, wearing the strapless blue dress that hits just below her knees. But the last time I told her what I think about her body things got out of hand. We both know we can't let that happen today. But it doesn't mean I'm not thinking about it.

"Stop deflecting. Talk to me for real, Gibson."

I sigh. "I've only been gone for a week and my mom's already redecorating my room. I didn't think I'd care. But it feels a little like they're trying to erase me. Plus, everything's about to change with Danielle getting married. It's just a lot, I guess."

Alice squeezes the arm she's still holding. "I get it."

"I know you do."

Alice nods and releases me. "I'm thrilled for them. I really am. But it's hard not to feel like we're losing her. Things won't be the same after this. We're growing up."

"Growing up kind of sucks." I laugh, looking down at her.

"It has its moments of pure suckage, for sure. But this isn't supposed to be one of them, so pep up. Let's go get our best friend married." Alice tugs on my hand, and I walk slower than necessary because I don't want her to let go.

We head outside and around to the backyard. Alice helps Danielle hold up the back of her dress as she glides across the grass my mom worked with the landscaping company all week to transform into something out of a Drew Barrymore movie. The ground is still a little damp, but everything else is perfect. Shelia Gibson would settle for nothing less. There's an outdoor dance floor and a huge tent set up on the side lawn to serve a buffet dinner. People are seated in rows of white chairs that are lined up facing out to the water, with an aisle of grass down the center. Down on the pier, rope lights are strung between the pilings. Danielle and Mike are both beaming, and I really am happy for them.

Mike is standing next to Jordan, and Edna Plum is on his other side as the officiant. They're waiting for us under a huge floral arch. Mike's parents and sisters are sitting in the front row, and Jordan is not being as subtle as he thinks he is with the way he keeps looking in their direction. Rodriguez is standing on the edge of the grass with a guitar. He sees Danielle, nods in our direction, and starts fingerpicking an Ed Sheeran song. Everyone in the chairs rises to their feet.

Regina's daughter, Emily, walks down the aisle first, tossing white petals as she makes her way to her mom in the front row. Then it's time for me to escort Alice down to the pier. She holds a bouquet of white and blue flowers in one hand and slides the other hand into the crook of my arm.

"You really do look good today, Ace," I whisper.

"You don't look so bad yourself." She squeezes my arm, and the faint scent of citrus floats up at me.

After the short ceremony, we all make our way to the catering tent. Mike and Danielle do their first dance, and then other guests take to the dance floor. Alice and I are seated together with the rest of the bridal party when one of Mike's cousins comes over to our table. He's the one with the hipster mustache who has been telling everyone within a three-table radius about his facial hair care routine and his plans to launch a new cryptocurrency targeted at teenage investors.

"You." He points at Alice. "Dance floor." He moves his shoulders with a slow shimmy that I think he intends to be attractive.

Dude is delusional if he thinks this strategy's going to work with her.

She plasters a big, fake smile on her face. "How flattering. But I'm afraid I'm not available. Jake here just asked me." She turns to me, her raised eyebrows begging me to go along with her story.

I will, but I'm not above having a little fun in the process.

"That's right. And now that Alice is *finally* out of the bathroom, we can get out on the dance floor. But only if you're feeling better, dear. Is the Pepto finally kicking in? It was really touch and go there for a while." I turn to the dude, who is looking confused, like he really thought ordering a stranger to spend time with him would produce better results.

To my surprise, Alice clutches her stomach and plays along. "You know, on second thought, I might need another minute."

I hold in a laugh and look at Cousin Mustache. "Might want to stay away from the crab balls. They aren't sitting well." He nods and shuffles away.

Alice laughs and goes back to eating her food. "Thanks for that."

"I do what I can. Do you actually want to get out there?" I point to the dance floor. "You know, with someone who won't talk about beard oil the entire time."

She plucks a green bean from her fork with her teeth. "Is that an invitation or just a general inquiry?" Even after everything that happened this week, she still wants to play hard to get?

I hold her gaze. "Will you dance with me, Alice?"

"One dance." She nods and removes the napkin from her lap, setting it on the table as she stands to follow me out to the floor.

In those heels Alice is taller than usual, and her head nearly reaches my shoulder. I put one hand on her waist and take her hand in the other. Neither of us says a word, but as the music plays we sway back and forth, drawing closer to each other one centimeter at a time, until her cheek is resting on the lapel of my suit jacket. Finally, I let go of her hand to wrap my arms fully around her.

Over the top of Alice's short curls, I see my mom glare at me and shake her head.

Chapter 17

Alice

I feel Jake's shoulders tense when he finally notices the nasty looks his mom's been shooting us since he sat down next to me for dinner. The song comes to an end, and as soon as he takes his hands away, I want them back. I know it's not smart, but I wish I could have him to myself again. Just the two of us. I'm thrilled for Danielle, I truly am. But I'm also ready to get away from Shelia's house.

Jake steps back and rubs a hand over his face.

"You look like you could use a break. Do you want to sneak out of here?" I stare up at him.

He shakes his head. "We probably shouldn't."

"Okay." I nod and start back to the table. The rejection stings, but he's right. We shouldn't ditch our best friend's wedding. And we both know what happened the last time we were alone.

Jake's hand darts out and wraps around my wrist. "Then again, they won't miss us if we're only gone for a few minutes."

I nod and follow him into the house.

He pulls me into the first doorway we see. It's a guest bedroom his parents are using as a coat check area. Purses and sweaters are scattered on the queen-sized bed, along with a few suit coats. I briefly wonder why he didn't have me sleep in here the night I hurt my ankle, but I decide it was probably because he didn't want it to look like he had a guest. We were hoping no one would find out he brought me home. Realizing we were hiding then just like we're hiding now doesn't feel good, but I shove the thought away just as my back hits the wall. Jake's hungry eyes stare down at me, looking for confirmation we're really doing this.

I raise one brow and try to pull off a seductive face. "Lovely wedding. Have you tried the cupcakes?"

He holds my gaze. "I can't stop thinking about those cupcakes."

"Me, neither." The words come out in a breathy whisper.

I don't know if it's the wedding hormones in the air or the memory of our time spent trapped in the cottage, but we both dive into each other at the same time. He grabs the back of my thighs and lifts me. I wrap my legs around him while our mouths crash together.

"No one can know about this," I insist.

"I know."

His hands tug at my hair, and I pull his shirt loose, running my fingers underneath it and along his rippled abs. I can feel the evidence of his attraction to me growing between us, and I know we should stop this. But I don't want to. Now that I know what he's offering, I want more. I grind against him and he groans into my mouth.

"Are you getting married today, too?" a tiny voice asks.

I pull back from Jake, and I'm horrified to see Emily standing in the doorway in her flower girl dress. Regina comes in right behind her.

"Let's just grab Mommy's purse and then— oh. Um, sorry." She looks at me, then a smile spreads across her face.

Jake ducks his head and chuckles into my neck. At least one of us thinks this is funny. Regina gives me two thumbs up, then grabs her purse quickly and hurries Emily out the door, which she shuts and locks behind her.

Jake and I couldn't even keep our hands to ourselves for three days. Now the secret's out. What are we doing?

Chapter 18

Alice

After finishing my latest Creative Writing assignment, I finally have time to focus on my own story again. I'm sprawled out on my bed in sweatpants and a sports bra, my laptop open and covered with potato chip crumbs, when I get a text.

Regina: OMG, girl. This book is fire! The scene in the grass? I cannot. I need to find a man to get down and dirty with me like that in real life.

I laugh.

Me: You and me both.

Regina: Something tells me you already found one.

Me: Hush. You know nothing.

Regina: You know I'd never tell a soul. But seriously, the book is great! The club should read it when it's released.

Me: That's literally my worst nightmare. It was hard enough to share it with you. Doesn't matter, though. This one might not even get to release at this point. But thanks. I needed to hear it.

Regina: What do you mean you won't release? Spill.

I groan, hopping up to shut my bedroom door because my dad has the volume on the TV turned up so loud I can hear every time a contestant presses their buzzer. I send her a voice memo to explain the problems I'm having. I need help updating the graphics on my website, and I also can't find a cover artist within my budget, which is basically non-existent. I'm not using stock images because the last time I did that someone with a huge social media following used the same photo and decided our books looked too similar. I'd never even heard of them, but they accused me of copying their work and sent a bunch of internet trolls after me. I never want to go through that again.

She responds with a three-word solution.

Regina: *Just ask him.*

It probably does seem that simple to her. After what she walked in on, I'm sure she thinks Jake and I are a thing.

We aren't.

At least I don't think we are. We haven't even spoken since the wedding. She's right, though, it would make sense to ask him. After all, before he left college he did go to school for graphic design and digital marketing, and he is the best artist in North Bay. But I can't call the guy I've been badmouthing for years and ask him to do me a favor right after I hooked up with him. Can I?

I turn back to my laptop screen and try to focus, but I can't concentrate on writing. I meant what I said to Regina. None of this is going to matter if I can't get these cover design and website issues sorted. Knowing all the work I put into the words, I never would have believed writing the book is the easiest part of writing a book. But it's true.

Regina's advice is pretty solid. I really should ask Jake about this. He would at least be able to point me in the right direction.

I let out a sigh and abandon the idea that I'm going to get any new words written today. Then I pick up my phone to text him.

Me: *Hey, can I talk to you about something?*

My phone rings immediately.

"Is everything okay?"

Hearing his voice enter my space shifts my equilibrium.

"Yeah." My mouth is suddenly dry. I can't remember the last time I spoke to Jake on the phone. I hold it against my shoulder and twist off the cap of the water bottle next to me. "It's nothing dramatic. I was wondering if I could, uh, hire you?"

"Hire me?"

"Yes. I find myself interested in your services." I take a sip and wait for him to speak. What is so difficult to understand about this?

"Like…as an escort? Is this your bizarre way of asking for a booty call?"

I spit out the water and start coughing. "What? No!" Does he really think I'm so hard-up for affection that I would offer to pay him for it? "I need someone to do some art for me. You do commissions, right?"

"Oh, sweet. What's the project?"

"A book cover. Maybe some help with my website? Possibly also separate character art?" The longer this conversation drags on, the less confident I feel.

"Can you send it to me?"

"No. Absolutely not."

Letting him read my book would be like letting him read my diary, only maybe worse. What if my writing is as bad as Ratnick thinks it is?

"Look, I can't draw you anything if I don't know what your book is about." Jake chuckles. The low, throaty sound transports me straight back to our time in the cottage and makes me shiver.

I take a breath. "Can I just tell you? It's about these women." I pause, trying to think of how I want to phrase my description. Why am I so embarrassed about this? I love this book. I worked hard on it.

"Okay…gonna need a little more than that."

"And they live together in this commune in a swamp. Their population is dying, and they need to find a way to preserve their way of life, but they don't necessarily want men to be part of their utopian society. So, they start a separate off-site area that is just for…procreation purposes. And then things start to get complicated with jealousy and power dynamics and stuff, which makes their community structure fall apart. But it's primarily a forbidden love story between the leader's daughter and one of the male concubines." I cringe and wait for him to laugh at me.

"Can I read it? Please?"

"Why?" I practically squeak. "I just told you everything you need to know."

"Mostly because you wrote a book, and that's awesome. But also because if you want me to create artwork for it, then I need to understand what I'm drawing."

"Oh." I'm the one asking for a favor, and I can't argue with his logic, so I give in. "Yeah. Fine. I'll email you a copy."

"Cool." A new text comes through with the email address he wants me to use.

"How much do you charge?" I ask, dreading his answer.

"Under normal circumstances, I would say it depends on the scope of the project."

"What kind of circumstances are these?"

"Exceptional ones." I can hear the smile in his voice. He's toying with me. He's either going to charge me double or think of something outrageous I need to do for him before he will agree to this.

"Exceptional how?"

"How do you feel about bartering services?" he asks. "My uncle asked me to ride out and take a look at a new property near Williamsburg this week. Do you want to come with me? We could get lunch or something while we're out there."

"Do you really think it's a good idea to go back to another empty house together?" But even as I say it, I can feel my own resolve crumbling.

"Presumptuous much?" he teases. "I could use another set of eyes on this property. I want to make sure I'm not overlooking anything major. And I thought it would be nice to have some company, that's all."

"Yeah. Okay," I agree. What harm could come from a little road trip and a lunch date with a friend?

Chapter 19

Alice

"Where do you want to eat after we look at the house?" Jake asks when he picks me up after my morning class on Wednesday.

I shrug. "Whatever you want is fine."

He's wearing a button-down shirt with the sleeves rolled up to expose his tattoos, and it's tucked into dark jeans. The addition of the belt is what makes me curious. Maybe he's only trying to look professional for the meeting with the real estate agent, but Jake almost never wears a belt. He's usually in athletic shorts or sweatpants. Honestly, I have no complaints about the sweatpants, but I also definitely don't mind this business casual look on him.

"Come on. Don't do that. Just tell me," he says.

"Do what? I don't know what you're talking about." We're already bickering, and we've only been alone together for like ten seconds.

I'm not in my normal clothes either. Typically, I wear leggings and a sweatshirt to class, but today I debated on my outfit for way too long before deciding on a lavender sundress. Because belts and sundresses scream "not a date," right?

"Why can't women ever decide where you want to eat? Is it that hard?"

From the way his eyes crinkle, I know Jake's only messing with me, but I'm already irritated. After having to sit through yet another class with Ratnick today, my patience is non-existent. "I don't know what kind of food options will be available where we're going. How am I supposed to be the one to choose?"

"What do you want, Alice? Do you even know?"

I scoff. I'm not even sure we're still talking about food. "Far be it from me to speak for my entire gender, but for me personally, it isn't so much not knowing what I want. It's more knowing you don't want to hear the real answer."

He smiles and raises his eyebrows. "Try me."

Maybe he really does like it when I get sassy with him. I'm happy to oblige. "It's like maybe what I really want is a Coke specifically from McDonald's, but then pizza for the actual meal, which they don't serve there. So maybe I want to order pizza from Formaggio's because they are the only ones with dairy-free cheese. But maybe I want something else for dessert. That's three separate places. And there's no way that anyone, including me, wants to run to three different restaurants for one meal. I wouldn't even do that if I were by myself."

"Okay, so what would you do if you were by yourself?"

"Realistically? Probably eat a coconut yogurt and some grapes. Then pop a bag of popcorn and watch bad reality TV. Maybe follow it up with some refrigerated cookie dough. Have you heard of girl dinner? It's a real thing. But again, that's not an option when you are trying to consider someone else."

"Why not?"

The first answer that pops into my head is *because that's not what people do on a date*. But I can't say that because we both know this is not a date.

"Because you're twice my size, and if we eat yogurt cups for lunch you'll be starving in an hour. Besides, you're probably one of those guys who thinks every meal has to have at least two dead animals in it." If he can make sweeping generalizations, so can I.

"What are you talking about?" Jake laughs.

"Oh, like you're not a bacon cheeseburger, meat lovers' pizza, or surf and turf kind of man?"

He blinks. "What does any of this have to do with you picking a restaurant?"

"Everything. You really don't get it, do you?"

He turns fully to look at me, amusement dancing in his eyes. "Please continue to enlighten me."

"Maybe all I want is a smoothie or a bowl of soup. Maybe I want to try a vegan place, but I know that's not your first choice and I don't want to pick something you're just going to whine about the entire time."

His smile widens, and he points at me. "There we go. We can work with that."

Before I know it, Jake is parking in front of a two-story brick colonial with a "for sale" sign in the front yard.

He exits the car and jogs around to open my door, but I'm fully capable of opening it for myself, so I get out before he reaches me.

The agent greets us at the front door.

"Hi, I'm Kevin. Thanks for coming out today. This house would make a wonderful home for a young couple like yourselves." He ushers us inside. Kevin is also wearing a belt with his khakis, which I take as confirmation that Jake dressed to meet with him and not me.

I open my mouth to insist we're not a couple, but Jake speaks first.

"Thanks for meeting us, we appreciate it." He puts his hand on the small of my back and leads me further into the house.

Kevin gives us space to look around. It's a big house with some cool architectural features, like the thick crown molding and curved stair rail, but it's outdated and smells musty. They must be getting ready to repaint the dining room, because the chairs are missing and the table is draped with a drop cloth that looks very familiar.

My eyes shift to Jake and he smirks, clearly sharing my fond memories of a similar piece of fabric. I follow him into the bathroom, where he sees some black spots on the ceiling and snaps a few photos to send his uncle.

"Is that mold?" I ask him, as he stands on the edge of the tub to get a closer look.

"Yeah. There's probably a lot more of it under this wallpaper, and on the way in I saw three cracks in the foundation. We're done here. It's not worth what they're asking, and I don't want my family to get into negotiations with people who didn't have the integrity to disclose this stuff in the first place."

I have to admit, it's pretty hot seeing him in full business mode.

"So that's it?"

"That's it. Sorry it wasn't more exciting. Are you ready for lunch?"

It's only a short drive before we park in front of a black building with an attached wooden pergola.

"Welcome to Root and Vine." We're greeted by a woman wearing a flowy jumpsuit and a long mermaid braid. Her thick, clear-framed glasses overwhelm her face, but in a way that seems like an intentional fashion choice.

"All our foods are locally sourced. Our specials change daily according to what's fresh. They're displayed on the chalkboard," she says as she escorts us to our table and gestures behind us.

The eight-foot-tall chalkboard covers an entire wall. It displays the specials in bright blues and pinks, and invites guests to add their own artwork underneath. There's a faded stick-figure in the corner, but otherwise no one has taken them up on the offer.

"Oh, I'm definitely hitting that up before we leave," Jake says as we are seated across from each other in a wooden booth. The hostess nods and leaves us to look over the menus, which advertise this place as "Virginia's premiere vegan restaurant."

I brace myself for Jake to complain, but he only says, "Sweet, they have cauliflower wings. What looks good to you?"

"I think I might get a salad so I can order a milkshake. It's been forever since I've been able to have one."

"Can't you just order what you actually want and get the milkshake anyway? Why do you have to eat a salad first?"

"Because bodies need vegetables and milkshakes aren't dinner."

"Says who? Besides, everything here is made out of plants. So, you're going to be eating vegetables no matter what."

"Says everyone. Don't you remember how we felt after eating only cupcakes for days? Those were vegan, too. But they weren't an actual meal. I don't want to spend the rest of the day with a stomachache and crashing from a sugar high."

"I told you, I definitely remember those cupcakes. And I, for one, liked how my body felt during those days. A lot." The knowing look he gives me makes my ears burn. "You don't want to just eat sugar? Fine. But you can get a salad anywhere. We came all the way out here. Try to live a little."

"Don't food shame me."

"Sorry. I'm not trying to. I just think we can get a little more creative than lettuce and carrots is all. There are only eight entrées listed. Let's order one of everything and share them."

I stare at him. I'm not sure if he's serious, but I argue anyway. "There's no way we'll ever be able to eat all of that. And I wouldn't want it to go to waste."

"We don't have to eat it all right now. We can get everything boxed up and take home whatever we don't eat. Come on. We're supporting a small business and boosting the local economy." He tilts his head and bats his eyes at me.

"Fine, you win," I relent. "But I'm paying for my fair share."

"I won the minute you agreed to come out with me in public, Ace." He winks.

"I guess that's true. You *are* fortunate I have chosen to grace you with my presence." I nod dramatically. "But we're going to need a double order of the cashew cheesecake, because I'm not sharing it."

"Deal."

I slide the menu up to hide my smile.

When our server returns, Jake explains his plan to order one of everything else on the menu and two pieces of cheesecake. She seems overwhelmed, but she's happy to grant the request.

"We'll take most of it to-go. But could you bring us two milkshakes and an order of cauliflower wings to start with here, please?" Jake asks.

"Sure thing. What flavors?"

I order strawberry and he goes for peanut butter swirl.

"It's gonna take a while. This is a big order," she warns.

"That's totally fine, we're not in a hurry." Jake smiles at her, and from the way she stutters trying to thank him, I can see his natural charm has her flustered. Girl, same.

When she shuffles away, Jake takes my hand and pulls me out of our booth toward the chalkboard. He draws a small squiggly line and hands me a piece of chalk.

"Your turn."

I remember this game from when we were kids. I add a circle to the top to make it look like a balloon. We take turns going back and forth. Each time I add a small line or shape Jake manages to expand it into something amazing. We continue adding to our drawing until it develops into an elaborate carnival scene, complete with a realistic-looking Ferris wheel and an elephant balancing a beach ball on its trunk. When our food is ready, we head back to our table.

By the time our bill arrives, it feels like hardly any time has passed. I look at my phone, and I'm surprised to see we've been here for almost two and a half hours.

"We better head out," I tell him.

Jake nods and starts to put our to-go containers into the bags our server provided.

As we pack up our food, I'm surprised at how reluctant I am to leave. I'm glad we still have more time in the car together, which is a far cry from how I felt about the long drive to the bakery just a few weeks ago.

I'm so full and content as Jake pulls back onto the highway that when my phone rings, I just want to ignore it. Even when I see my dad's name, my first inclination is to let it go to voicemail like I usually do. But I pick it up.

"Yeah, Dad? What do you need?"

I hear him wheeze on the other end of the line, but he doesn't say anything.

"Dad?" I repeat. "Dad. Answer me. What's going on?"

Still nothing.

Jake looks at me from the driver's seat. Concern creases his brow.

"Something's wrong. Can I use your phone?" Only half the words leave my mouth before he hands it to me.

"0421," he tells me his passcode.

I put my own phone on my thigh and try three times to correctly punch the numbers into his with my shaking hands, but I can't do it, and Jake's phone locks me out.

"It's okay," he assures me softly. You can still hit the emergency call icon."

"Why didn't you say that in the first place?" I snap at him before offering a quick, "Sorry. I know this isn't your fault."

Jake nods. His eyes are soft.

My heart pounds harder with each moment that passes without a response on the other end of my line. I press the emergency button on Jake's phone and switch mine to speaker. "Dad, stay on the phone with me. I'm driving home with a friend, but we are still pretty far away. I'm calling an ambulance to come check on you."

He grunts, then coughs, and I listen until I hear him take a shaky breath.

A little wave of relief washes over me, but it's short-lived while I think about all the things that could be wrong. Is he having a heart attack or a stroke? Or maybe he fell and hit his head. All the maybes and what-ifs pile on top of each other until they form a solid ball of dread deep in my gut.

"911. What's your emergency?"

I swallow. Then I try to stop from shaking as I put the phone to my ear and tell the operator everything I know so far, which isn't much.

Jake sets a hand on my knee while the dispatcher says she is sending an ambulance. She instructs me to stay on the line and to try to keep my dad calm until the first responders arrive.

"Okay," I speak into both phones, not sure who I'm saying it to. "Dad, the ambulance is on the way."

My stomach lurches. I know it can take a long time for them to get out to rural areas like ours.

Jake motions for me to hand his phone back. He doesn't hang up with the dispatcher, but he sends off a quick series of texts. I want to yell at him to keep his eyes on the road, but I'm too overwhelmed by the fog of anxiety surrounding me to argue. In fact, I'm having trouble saying much of anything. A lump clogs my throat and tears well in my eyes as I suck in short, shallow breaths.

Jake finishes his texts and places his phone back in my lap. "Mr. Caulfield," he says, "this is Jake Gibson. I'm here with Alice. We'll meet you at the hospital. We've already called for help, and they're coming, but it will take a while to get to you. In the meantime, my roommate and a few members of the baseball team are going to stop by, okay?" He turns to me and lowers his voice slightly. "At least they're trained in First Aid and CPR. They'll be right there."

"How?" I finally find my voice.

"I knew Jordan was around, so I texted him. He said he's with some of the guys, and they're going to head over to see what's going on. They're close. He'll get back to us with an update in a few minutes. Breathe, Ace."

I reach over and touch Jake's arm. "Thank you."

He nods and takes my hand, linking his fingers with mine. "Of course." His firm grip is grounding.

I did not have holding hands with Jake while we rush toward my dad's medical emergency on my bingo card for this year, but here we are.

"Any minute now, Mr. Gibson. Hang in there." Jake continues to talk to my dad through the speaker as though they are old friends, even though Dad isn't saying anything back to him.

Finally, we hear some shuffling.

"We're here," Jordan's voice lets us know he's arrived. "He's sitting on the ground on the front porch. I don't see any visible injuries, but Ashley's going to check him out."

Jake explains that their pitcher's girlfriend happens to be a nurse. She's there with them to look him over.

"I'm going to hang up now and video call you right back so you can see him," Jordan says. When he does, I see Dad sitting with his back against our front door. He's looking pale, and Ashley has her fingers on his neck while she looks at her watch.

After she stops counting, Ashley turns to the camera. "We'll stay right here with him until the ambulance arrives," she reassures me.

"Thanks, guys," Jake says. "We know he's in good hands."

I nod and wipe my eyes.

But the relief doesn't last long before a landslide of guilt and regret hits. I should have been there. I shouldn't have left my dad alone.

Jake squeezes my hand. "It's going to be okay."

I give him a small half-smile, but my heart sinks. He doesn't know that.

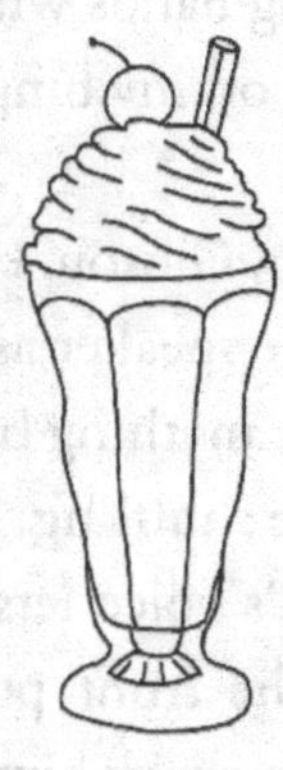

Chapter 20

Jake

We got to the hospital as quickly as we could. It looks like Mr. Caulfield had a mild heart attack. He'll need to stay here for a few days so they can run more tests and observe him, but then they think he should be able to return home.

I can tell Alice is freaking out as she paces the family waiting area. She's keeping it close to the chest, but I can see the fear in her eyes, and the tension is radiating off her. She's already lost one parent, and now the other is lying in a hospital bed.

I take a few steps toward her. "Do you want to stay here with him tonight? I can bring you your car in the morning." My hand hovers halfway between us, but I put it down because I don't know how she'll react to being touched.

"I know he doesn't want me to be here. He doesn't like people seeing him weak like this. The nurse said he's stable enough that it would be okay if I went home to sleep and shower before tomorrow." Alice takes a deep breath and lets all the air out at once. "It's going to be a long few days, and my dad is a bear at the best of times."

"Well, the good news is, we don't need to worry about dinner," I say, which causes her to huff out a reluctant laugh. There's enough food to feed the entire baseball team in the backseat of my car.

Inching closer to her, I test the waters and hold out my arms. Right now, she might be just as likely to bite my head off as she is to accept a hug. But she leans in and lets me close my arms around her. It could be my imagination, but I think she's even squeezing back a little.

"Let's get you home," I tell the top of her head.

"Yeah. Okay. Thanks."

She's quiet for the whole ride back to her house.

"You don't have to come in," she says when we pull into the gravel driveway. "I'll be fine."

"Alice. Your dad just had a heart attack. I'm not leaving you alone. Besides, we need to get all the food inside."

She sighs. "Just…try not to judge the place too much, okay? He's been sick."

"Of course." I rest a hand on her thigh and use my other hand to turn her face toward mine. "I don't care what your house looks like. I'm not here for decorating ideas. I'm here for you."

She goes quiet again for a minute, then she nods and gets out of the car. "Okay. But don't say I didn't warn you."

I gather the bags and follow behind her.

It's been forever since I've been inside the Caulfields' home. It's a small two-bedroom cottage on the outskirts of town, not unlike Uncle Tim's rental, except Alice's house has never been updated and it's showing its age. Walking up to the house now feels like the beginning of a zombie movie. All the flower beds are dead, and there are cobwebs on every corner of the porch. There's a tear in the screen door, and it creaks loudly as Alice pulls it open. She winces as we step inside.

"Looks like the storm did some damage here," I say, trying to give her dad the benefit of the doubt. There's no pride of ownership in this property anymore, but I know it hasn't always been like this. Their family never had much, but when Mrs. Caulfield was here it was clean and well-kept. Tulips bloomed in front of the concrete porch every spring, and she was always cooking something in her extremely tidy kitchen. Obviously, that's no longer the case.

"Don't make excuses for him. This place is a disaster." She sighs and turns to me. "I haven't had anyone besides Danielle over in a really long time, and even she doesn't come around much anymore. It's a lot different than it used to be."

I take her hand and squeeze it. "Hey. We're all different than we used to be. That's not always a bad thing. And I'm not afraid of a little bit of dust."

She leads me into the main area where the living room, dining room, and kitchen are all segmented into their own small spaces. There are piles of vehicle parts stacked in every corner, motor oil stains on the floor, and trash littered everywhere. It's like an episode of Hoarders and an episode of Junkyard Wars collided and crash-landed here.

"I'm so sorry. You just wanted some company to look at that house, and now you're stuck in this mess with me."

I put one finger over her lips.

"Don't do that. I'm not stuck. I want to be here. Put me to work. I have it on pretty good authority that you like bossing me around."

"I don't even know where to start…" Alice starts to talk, then her voice trails off.

"Okay, so you don't have to do anything yet. I'll put the food in the fridge. You rest. It's been a long day."

She nods and hugs her hands around her midsection, but she doesn't move. Her eyes scan the room, and tears start to pool in them again.

"Let's take a minute and sit on the porch," I suggest. "You were looking forward to that cheesecake, right? We'll have a picnic for dessert. Then we can come back in here and do a little bit of tidying up, if you want. But this isn't your mess, Alice. You aren't responsible for it."

"That's the thing, though. I am responsible. Because if I don't do it, then no one else will." The hurt in her voice is cracking my heart in half.

"Here. Let's go outside and get some cheesecake in you. Then I'll stay here all night and clean with you if you want."

Alice closes her eyes and takes a few breaths. When she opens them again, she looks up at me. "This is so embarrassing. I feel like such a failure."

"Why? You didn't cause this."

"My mom made me promise to take care of him, and I…" She chokes on a hiccup and starts blinking rapidly. "I just…can't. I'm trying. I really am, but…" She spreads out her arms and gestures at the mess. "It builds up so much faster than I can control it." Then the tears come.

I can't do anything but listen, and it kills me. It's like she's tearing her way into my chest with those bright orange fingernails and slicing my heart to shreds. I want to fix this for her, but I don't know if I can.

"Listen, your mom was really special, and I'm so sorry she's gone, but I'm pretty sure she didn't mean this. She wouldn't want to put that on you. She loved you. And you're the kid in this situation, not the parent."

Alice nods and sniffles. "Thank you. I think I needed to hear that. But I still feel so guilty. I mean, she always had this place clean and looking cute, so I know it can be done, but I obviously suck at it."

I take her face in my hands and tilt it up while I use my thumbs to brush away some of her tears. "Stop. It's not the same. She had responsibilities. And so does your dad. She was his wife and a mother. He's the owner of this house. You are none of those things. This isn't your job. I can stay and help, and we can try to make this place a little better for your dad, but you can't make him change any more than anyone else can. You don't have to be your mom. You can just be you. That's enough."

"Is it, though?"

"Yes. Dammit, Alice. You're more than enough."

She scoffs at that. "You really don't need to do this."

"Yeah, I do. Because you need to hear it. You deserve so much better than this. I'm sorry I haven't been good at showing you that. But I'm here now, and I'm in this with you. For real."

"I don't know what that means, Jake. I don't know if I can make you the same kind of promise right now."

"You've got enough on your plate tonight. We don't need to talk about labels for whatever is happening here." I wave my hand between us. "All I'm saying for now is you deserve a break. I wish I had one of those ancient stretcher things to carry you on while you get fanned with giant leaves and eat grapes or something, but I don't. So, instead, we're going to sit out on that porch and eat your weird cashew cheesecake. Then we're going to scrub the toilet together or whatever else needs to be done."

She purses her lips and starts to roll her eyes at me, but then her face softens. "Thank you. I don't know what I did to deserve it, but I'm glad you're with me today."

I hug her again. "I wouldn't be anywhere else."

Chapter 21

Alice

Jake puts the food away in the kitchen, except for the two boxes of cheesecake. Then we walk out to the porch. He sits next to me on the top step, close enough that our shoulders touch as he hands over my box.

Anxiety has stolen my appetite, but I open the packaging and pick up the plastic fork the restaurant included.

"I don't know if I can eat," I admit.

Jake nods and gently takes the fork from me. He uses it to break off a small piece of the cake and bring it to my lips. "It's been a long time since lunch. Will you try?" he asks. "Just a little bit. Please?"

I open just enough for him to slide in a bite. He gives me a soft smile.

I feel my phone buzz in my pocket, and when I pull it out, Danielle's name and photo are on the screen.

I sigh. I don't know if I'm ready to talk to anyone else, but Jake gives me another nod of encouragement.

"Hey," I answer.

"Oh my God! Jordan told Mike an ambulance was called to your dad's place. Tell me everything. We've been waiting to hear from you. How's Earl? What do you need? Are you at the hospital? If you're home now, we can be at your place in ten minutes."

As I listen, I find myself smiling for the first time in a while. No matter what life decides to throw at me, I can always count on Danielle and Honey. And now, apparently, Jake.

"Dad was admitted to the hospital. It was his heart. He'll be there for a few days. Actually, if you're up for it, I could really use some help getting the house in shape. I hate to ask, but I can't do it alone. And I want to try to clean it up a bit before he gets home."

"Of course we're up for it," Danielle says.

"Wild horses couldn't stop us!" Honey yells in the background.

"I doubt wild horses could stop Honey Daniels from doing anything," I muse.

"Damn straight!" Honey yells again.

"We'll get some supplies together and head over soon," Danielle tells me before we hang up.

A little bit more of the tension leaves my body, and I give Jake a shy smile while I take a few more bites. He nudges my shoulder playfully, and I retaliate by lightly pinching his side.

"Where should we start?" he asks once we finish our cheesecake.

I stand up and scan the property. The garden could use tending and the grass is dead, but there's not much point in starting outside. "Um, how do you feel about washing the dishes in the sink while I strip his bed and start some laundry? And then we'll need to clear things out so he can get around."

"On it." Jake stands up and clears our picnic, then goes inside.

I stay on the porch for another minute until Honey's car pulls up. Danielle flies out of the passenger's seat to wrap me in a hug. In her denim overalls over a sports bra, with a bandana tied over a French braid, she certainly looks like she came to work.

"The cavalry has arrived," Honey announces as she exits the car and reaches into the back seat. "I brought supplies and sustenance." She holds a broom in one hand and a container of soup in the other. "Alice, you march inside and sit yourself down. You've had a hard day. Put your feet up for a minute."

I'm afraid if I sit down again, I'll fall apart and never be able to get my momentum back, so I just say, "I'm okay. I think keeping busy might help."

Honey nods and heads inside, and Danielle and I follow. Honey goes straight to the kitchen, where she hip-checks Jake out of the way and starts barking orders.

"I can do these dishes. Why don't you put those fancy muscles to use and start moving some of these car parts to clear space?" she says to Jake, then turns to me. Her glasses are fogging from the hot water as she pulls on a pair of yellow rubber gloves. "Maybe we can put the metal things all together on the screen porch out back?"

I'm grateful for her taking charge so I don't have to think. "Yeah, the car parts are important to him. We shouldn't get rid of anything besides obvious trash, I guess." There's plenty of that laying around.

Danielle scans the living room. "Wow. It's been a while since I've been here. I don't remember your dad's collection being quite this big," she tells me before calling out to her other bestie. "Hey, Jake."

She gives him a wave. If she wonders why he was already here, she doesn't ask.

"I know. It's gotten pretty out of hand."

"Nothing we can't handle together, I'm sure. I'll go start on the bathroom," she offers. Then we all get to work.

Honey blasts Hall and Oates on the old record player and finishes washing and putting up the dishes. Jake clears enough space for me to actually be able to run the vacuum. I honestly can't remember the last time that happened. When everyone has finished their jobs, we reconvene in the living room.

"I'm never going to be able to thank you all enough for this," I tell them as I switch off the vacuum cleaner. "I don't know how I could have handled all of this by myself."

"Don't be ridiculous," Honey says. "You'd never have to. This is what family is for. You'll never be alone in times like this as long as any of us are breathing. Ain't that right?" she prompts.

"Of course." Danielle smiles and squeezes the top of my arm.

"Yes ma'am," Jake answers Honey, then he looks into my eyes with a sincerity that is so real it makes me nervous. "We've got you, Ace."

Danielle tilts her head at the new nickname, but before she can question it we're interrupted by a knock on the door.

"Now, don't get angry, Sugar," Honey tells me. "But this job needs a few extra hands, so I called Mike, and he's coming over with Jordan."

"Hey, Alice."

"Sorry to hear about Earl," the guys greet me.

Regina lets herself in a few minutes later, holding a casserole dish in one hand and Emily's hand in the other.

"I called Regina, too," Danielle admits.

Emily briefly wraps her arms around my legs in a quick hello. "Can I draw on the porch with my sidewalk chalk?"

"Sure. I bet your pictures will help to cheer up my dad. He's been sick."

"I know. Mommy told me he was in the hospital."

"That's true, he is. But the doctors said he should be able to come home soon."

Once Emily scurries out to the porch, Regina reaches out with her now-free hand to touch my elbow.

"How are you holding up?" She walks over to the kitchen and opens the fridge. "I brought a pasta bake, but from the looks of all the takeout containers in here, it seems like you might be set for food."

"Thank you. This is so thoughtful, I'll put it in the freezer for Dad. You won't believe where all the rest of this came from." I relay the story in a hushed whisper. I'm almost glad she caught me with Jake at the wedding because it's nice to have someone to tell.

"What, did he order the entire menu?" she jokes, reopening the fridge to count the containers.

"Yes. That's exactly what he did. Thank you for not saying anything about what you saw."

"I haven't the faintest idea what you're referring to." Regina winks at me and laughs. "Now tell me, where can I be the most help?"

"Honestly, I'm not even sure where to begin with the rest of this mess. There's just so much to get rid of, but it's too much for us to haul to the dump ourselves."

"You know, Clark Davis has that hauling business now. You should call him. I bet this would be no problem for him," Regina says.

"That's a good idea. Do you have his number?"

"Oh, um, no, I don't actually know him very well." She tucks a dark curl behind her ear and breaks eye contact. "But I could ask around for you."

"If you need to talk to Davis, I'm sure Mike or Jordan can put you in touch with him," Jake says as he stops in the kitchen entrance with an armful of metal. "Want me to get you his number?"

"Yes, please," Regina says, a little too quickly.

"That would be great." I nod.

"Right. Please. You know. For Alice. Because she needs to talk to him." Regina's ears turn red.

Jake gives me an inquisitive look, but I just shrug. Regina is staying out of our business, and I'm staying out of hers.

Chapter 22

Alice

It was great to have so much help, but I'm relieved to finally be alone once Danielle, Mike, and Honey pull out of the driveway. They stayed later than everyone else. Jake asked if I wanted to go back to his apartment, so I wouldn't have to be alone, but I turned down the offer. I sent him home, along with Jordan, Regina, and Emily, a little while ago. Danielle makes heart-shaped hand gestures out the window of their car, and I wave as I close the door.

I insisted they should go, but now the house feels too empty. Hours of cleaning have left me sweaty and thirsty, so I head to the fridge in search of a drink. When I open the door, a dozen pairs of eyes stare back at me. I yelp in surprise, then I start to laugh. There are googly eyes stuck on almost every item in the refrigerator. I know exactly who did this.

I snap a photo and pour myself a glass of sweet tea before I set to work peeling them off. It's pretty adorable, but it made me jump, and I'm not trying to give Dad another heart attack when he gets home. I save one of the larger pairs and stick it on my laptop case. I chuckle as they stare back at me, and I send the photo to Jake.

Me: *I *see* what you did there.*

Jake: *Someone had to keep an *eye* on you tonight. ::wink emoji::*

He's such a dork. I'm still looking down at his message and smiling as I curl under the blanket and pull up a new document for my next Creative Writing assignment. But I can't concentrate because my fingers are itching to text Jake again. It would be so easy to ask him to come back and use those talented hands to make me forget all this stress. I can't do that, though. I don't want trauma bonding to become our thing. First the storm, and now we've spent another intense day together because of a health emergency. I don't want to come off needy and desperate.

Instead, I text Danielle.

Me: *I don't know the protocol now that you're an old married lady, but I think I made a mistake sending you away. How would you feel about coming back over here for an impromptu sleepover?*

Danielle: *Mike's already asleep. We wore him out. I won't be missed. Be there in fifteen.*

After two Kate Hudson movies and a bottle of wine, we are stretched sideways across my bed, talking about almost anything except the secret I'm now keeping from my best friend. The confession has been on the tip of my tongue all night. I might've slipped and told her by now if I could get a word in, but thankfully Danielle has been ranting about her movie icks since *Fool's Gold* ended.

"You know something else that bothers me about most movies?" There are way too many s's in that sentence. Danielle was never much of a partier, but now that she lives in a dry house, her tolerance is even lower. The wine has made her a little tipsy.

"What?"

"The complete omission of bodily functions," she slurs, but only slightly. "Like, I'm supposed to believe this group of people are together on all these adventures and not once did anyone need to pee? None of these women get their periods? Nobody farts, at all, ever?"

I laugh. "My professor calls those things 'gratuitous distractions.' He says it pulls the reader out of the story and cheapens the work."

She blows raspberries and little droplets of spittle hit my comforter. "Well, if you ask me, it's way more distracting to spend the entire time wondering if I'm watching humans or cyborgs because none of the characters seem to have a bladder."

I'm happy to join her on this crusade for cinematic justice. It's a much safer topic than a certain tattooed hottie we both know and love. Well, not *love*. I don't love Jake. That would be insane.

But I know I should tell her.

I gather my courage and say, "Believe me, bodily functions were top-of-mind when I was stuck with Jake. My intestines can't thank you enough for ordering vegan cupcakes."

"Are you kidding? I felt so bad that my insistence you get those cupcakes was the whole reason you both got stuck out there. I'm still shocked you didn't kill each other. But maybe it was good for you? Seems like you two are getting along much better now." My best friend looks at me with one eyebrow arched, waiting for my story.

She's handing me the perfect opportunity, so of course I completely chicken out. I want to tell her everything, but telling her will make it real, and I don't know if I'm ready for something as real as it could be with Jake. Or if he is. So instead of telling her the truth, I cop out and give her the most generic answer of all time.

"Yeah. We talked some stuff out. It's not like there was much else to do."

"I'm so happy you two are friends again." She leans back into my pillow.

I nod and turn the conversation back to her. "I'm happy you're happy. And I know you really are. I can see it. You're glowing, Mrs. Miller. I've never seen you look this good. Tell me about married life. How is it being a newlywed?"

She beams. "It's amazing. He's amazing. Everything is—"

"Let me guess. Amazing?"

She touches her finger to her nose, then points to me. "You're pretty smart, you know."

"I know. I'm a genius. You know what else? I think I've decided *Almost Famous* is Kate's best work."

"That was never in doubt." Danielle clinks her glass against mine and starts another movie.

Chapter 23

Jake

Saturday morning my body is telling me I could use another three or four hours of sleep, but I drag myself out of bed when the alarm goes off because I need to get over to the library. The first art class I'm teaching is today.

When I pull up to the old brick building, I notice Mrs. Caulfield's memorial garden is looking a little overgrown, so I take a minute to pluck a handful of weeds before heading inside. Mike's wrapping up his recovery meeting as I come in.

"I'll be out of your way in a second, let me just grab our signs," he says.

"It's cool, no rush. My class doesn't start until ten. But hey, while we're here, can I ask you something?"

Mike nods the go-ahead while he folds a wooden easel.

"When do you know it's time to step in and get involved if someone is self-destructing?"

He stops messing with the signs and straightens up to look at me. "Everything okay?"

You'd think I'd be used to it by now, but it still shakes me up when he does that. I'm not used to other guys being all direct with me about feelings. We certainly never talked about stuff like this in my house.

"Yeah, I'm good. I mean, things could be better with my parents, but that's not why I'm asking. Just trying to help a friend."

Mike nods. I'm sure he knows exactly who I'm talking about, but I don't know how much Danielle has told him about Alice's dad.

"I really wish I could tell you, man. It's different for everybody. Some people are in a place to be able to accept help, others aren't there yet. All you can do is listen and point them in the right direction. They have to start taking the steps themselves. The folks who come to my meetings need the same thing. We can give them information and help them find resources. After that, it's up to them."

"Okay." I take a breath. "What resources are those?"

"I have to warn you, there aren't a lot. It's been the one downside I've found to living in North Bay. Access to any kind of mental health services is really limited." Mike shakes his head. "If your friend was in the military, maybe try calling the Department of Veterans' Services? They might be able to help. But fair warning, if you find somewhere, it will probably be a ways away."

"That's a good idea. Thanks."

He nods and pats my shoulder with his free hand as he walks out with the easel tucked under one arm. There are still twenty minutes before my animation class begins, so as I set markers and paper on the tables, I make a call.

As our start time approaches, footsteps in the doorway cause me to turn from the whiteboard where I've been sketching a welcome cartoon. I turn, expecting to see my first student, but instead, Alice is walking toward me.

"What are you doing here, Ace? I thought you needed to be back at the hospital this morning. How's your dad?"

"I got to talk to him earlier. He's doing much better, but they're running more tests, so I can't see him until the afternoon. I'm headed there next, but I needed to see this. You're an art teacher now! That's kind of a big deal."

I scoff. "I'm volunteering at a library. Not exactly the same thing. I'm still the same dropout I was last week."

"Don't do that. This is great, Jake. Can I help? I can pass out papers or whatever. As a thank you for yesterday."

"You can stay if you want, but you don't owe me anything. I meant it when I said I'm glad I was there."

She slides into a chair in the back of the room and watches as the teenagers start to file in. It's actually a lot of fun to see how engaged they are while I show them how to draw a few of their favorite cartoon characters. Then I teach them how they can create different expressions by changing the shape of the eyebrows. I begin handing out dry-erase markers and laminated sheets of eyebrowless faces, and Alice stands to help, smiling as she takes the supplies from me.

"Is this your girlfriend?" The girl with braids asks. Next time, I need to bring nametags.

"This is Ms. Alice," I announce to the class, not taking my eyes off her. "She came to help today."

"I don't need help with that expression," the boy in the red shirt pipes up, pointing at me. "That's for sure the 'wants to bone her' face."

I turn to tell him that's completely inappropriate, but one of the girls is already scolding, "Don't talk to the teacher like that, Mason. He's cool." Another kid tosses a crumpled piece of paper at his head. "Besides, they're adorable together," the girl continues. "I totally ship this." She motions between me and Alice.

"That's enough, back to work." Alice smiles at them, and I think I see her give the girl a wink.

When our hour is up, Alice stays behind and giggles to herself as she helps me clean up. It doesn't take us long to toss the markers and leftover paper into a box.

"What?" I ask when she laughs again.

"Oh, nothing. I just didn't realize you'd be quite so popular. They really like you. Did you see the note they were passing around?"

"No. What did it say?"

"Well, one kid did call your shoes dumb. But otherwise, it was just a standard drool fest."

I briefly glance down at my shoes and shrug, then I smile at her. "Hazard of the job. People can't help falling in love with me."

"You wish. It's a pretty face, I'll give you that. Too bad it's hiding a complete lack of personality." She pushes me playfully.

"All I heard was you think I'm pretty." I laugh and hesitate before changing the subject. "So, I was talking to Mike a little bit before you got here. He pointed me in the direction of some services for veterans, and I made some calls." I pause to gauge her reaction, but it's unreadable. "I got a number for a therapist that accepts military insurance, if that's what your dad has. I'm not sure how all that works." I pull a torn scrap of paper from my pocket and hand her the information I jotted down. "I just wanted to help. If he decides to make an appointment, I can drive him. You don't have to do this alone, Alice."

Her hand comes up to cover her mouth. "Jake," she whispers my name through her fingers while she looks down at the note. Then she reaches out to touch my forearm. "This might literally be the nicest thing anyone's ever done for me."

"It's really not a big deal."

It was one phone call, and it probably only took five minutes. I was nervous to bring it up, but her soft, shining eyes tell me this was the right thing to do. She has no idea the lengths I'd go to in order to keep her looking at me that way.

Chapter 24

Alice

I read your book. Jake's maddening text has been staring back at me all afternoon. I mean, what am I supposed to do with that information? Concern burns my cheeks, because if he liked it, he would have said so, right? But I guess he isn't saying he didn't like it either.

Finally, I take a deep breath and pull up my big girl pants to type.

Me: *And?*

Jake: *Is there anything specific you're looking for with the cover?*

My stomach drops. He hated it. If he's really not going to share a single thought about the book that has been consuming every second of my free time for the past eight months, he must've thought it was terrible. How is this man tearing my insides apart while doing absolutely nothing?

Or not nothing, really. I suppose he's being professional. The cover is why I hired him. It's not like I asked for a book review. So, why does it feel like he's punishing me by withholding his opinion?

Screw this. I'm just going to ask.

Me: *What did you think?*
Jake: *About the book?*

Is he trying to make me beg? What else would I be talking about?

Jake: *Or the artwork?*

Oh. Right.

Me: *Well, both. But let's start with the book.*
Jake: *Can you come over? Not gonna write a dissertation via text. We can talk about it, and I'll show you some sketches.*

My keys are in my hand before I finish reading his message, and before I know it, I find myself buzzing to be let into his building and climbing the stairs to his apartment. I knock lightly, and Jake appears. He's wearing dark sweats and an old T-shirt advertising some event hosted by his former fraternity.

I came to this apartment a few times with Danielle back when Mike lived here. The small main living area still looks exactly the same. The only difference is the overstuffed dog bed in the corner. Hazel lounges with her head on her front paws, looking bored. When I coo a greeting at her, she lifts her head and yawns. She lets me scratch under her chin, then she flops back down again.

There's an open pizza box sitting on the kitchen counter. Veggie with no cheese. Only one half has pineapple.

"You remembered." I smile at him.

"I remember a lot of things." Jake hands me a plate and a glass of water. He motions for me to grab myself a slice while he takes a pineapple-free piece. "I've been thinking about your story," he says through a mouthful.

"Yeah?" I try not to let on how nervous I am to hear what he has to say.

"I started a few sketches, but before I finish, I need to know if we're on the same page. I want to make sure my vision for this matches the way you see these characters. What are you trying to evoke?"

"That sounds very esoteric and artsy. Much like the word *esoteric* itself." I don't even know what I'm talking about anymore. My brain is all scrambled because he's close enough for me to smell his body wash. I swallow. "I'm not sure I get what you mean."

"Let's start with this: why do you write? I assume it's not to get a good grade and a pat on the head from some douche professor."

"Of course not. I do it because I have to."

Jake puts his pizza down and looks into my eyes. He stays quiet, holding space for me to work out my own thoughts.

I've never thought about why I do it, it's just something I've always done. It's a part of my fabric. Before I knew how to hold a pencil correctly, I was making up plays to perform for my mom or crafting elaborate scenes for my stuffed animals.

"If I don't write, I don't know who I am," I tell him. "Sometimes I hear people talking about things like politics or pop culture, and I honestly don't know my own opinion until I sit down and write a journal entry to wade through my thoughts. Writing is how I discover what I think about the world, or work through the tough stuff."

When my mom was sick, I spent a lot of time alone with my journal.

"That's how I feel about drawing. Like, I walk around looking at stuff all the time, but in order to draw it, I have to take the time to sit down and really see everything about it. I need to notice the shapes, and the lines, and the way the light hits. Or the imperfections."

"You're good at that, seeing things other people don't." Like right now. I'm sitting here with him, talking about our art in a way I don't get to do with anyone else, eating the pizza he ordered because he remembered the way I like it. Jake makes me feel seen.

His eyes scan my face and land on my lips. "Thanks. So are you. There were a lot of little details in your writing. I tried to capture some of them." He uses his thumb to lightly brush the corner of my mouth. "You had a crumb."

I freeze and stare back at him. His hand stays hovering at my cheek, and for a moment it's like we're back at the cottage, alone with the familiar electric current traveling from his skin to mine.

Jake breaks the spell when he clears his throat and gets back to business. "There was a lot of commentary in your story about societal norms I never really thought about before. Let me show you what I have for the art so far." He wipes his mouth with a napkin, and he stands to grab his sketchbook from the coffee table. Then he motions for me to join him on the couch. I clear our plates and wash my hands before I sink into the cushion next to him. He flips a few pages and places the open book on my lap.

The pencil sketch he's drawn makes me gasp. "Jake, this is gorgeous."

It's a picture of my battle scene in the swamp done in intricate detail, down to the veins in every blade of grass. The characters are dressed exactly how I described, including the crest on my main character's armor. The face staring back at me from the page looks a lot like my own. And she's beautiful. Angry, fierce, and ready to fight for what she wants, but the first thing that comes to mind is she's beautiful. Is this how he sees me?

I turn the page, and I'm greeted with another scene pulled directly from my imagination and brought to life on paper. Then another. Six in total. The last one is from the love scene I was so nervous to have him read. He drew an aerial view that only shows the back of the male main character's head. His body is draped in a sheet as he hovers over his love, but her face— my face—is in full view as she reaches up to him. Her expression is adoring and serene. She looks peaceful and content wrapped in that sheet with him. The same way I must have looked at Jake that night in the cottage.

Emotion clogs my throat and I bring my hand up to cover my mouth. "This is…I don't know what to say."

"You like them?" There's a boyish hint of vulnerability in his question.

I lift my eyes to find him already staring at me, waiting for my answer.

My voice comes out breathy. "I love them." I nod at him, then I motion to the picture in my lap. "This one's my favorite."

For the first time, his returning smile is shy. It makes me think maybe he was as nervous to show me these as I was to have him read my story. He leans in to take back the book, and his hand brushes mine. His face is only inches away, and it continues to come closer until his lips are at my ear.

"I drew that one from memory," he whispers.

I shiver and swallow the moan that wants to escape. He's right here, barely a breath away. It would be so easy to turn to him and take what I want. But I freeze. I don't know if I can trust that these feelings are real. Or that they'll last. Back at the cottage, he said he likes Sassy Alice, but he's only had to deal with me in small doses so far. What if more will be too much for him?

Jake tucks a strand of hair behind my ear and puts his forehead to mine. "I feel you thinking too hard in there, Ace. Come back to me."

I close my eyes and try to find my words again, but then we hear footsteps.

"Sweet, you ordered pizza?" Jordan pads into the kitchen and makes a beeline for the box.

Jake straightens up and clears his throat before answering, "Uh, yeah. Help yourself." He runs a hand through his hair.

"Why does this have an entire salad on top of it?" Jordan asks.

I shake myself out of the trance those pictures and their artist put me in. "That would be because of me."

"Oh. Hey, Alice." Jordan raises a hand to greet me.

I stay for a little while, and we teach Jordan how to play Speed, but all too soon it starts to get late, and I need to get home. My dad is getting released from the hospital tomorrow.

Chapter 25

Jake

"Want to play Madden?" Jordan asks as he picks up the video game case.

"Sure."

"Huh. It got mixed up with Grand Theft Auto somehow." He pulls the wrong game out of the case and finds the GTA cover so he can switch them back. Except when he opens that one, he finds the Mario Party cartridge. Jordan tilts his head at me. "Is this like your one roommate flaw? Did we finally find it? You share your food and keep your room clean, but you don't know how to put your games back in the right cases?"

I groan. "Dammit. This has Alice written all over it."

He laughs. "You think she did this when she was here the other night? Why would she bother?"

"We've got this prank war going where we do little things to get under each other's skin. Nothing serious, just harmless but annoying stuff. Like this. I thought we'd called an unspoken truce, but apparently not."

Jordan nods. "I see. First-grade playground rules still apply."

I narrow my eyes and shake my head.

He laughs again. "What are you going to do next, pull her pigtails to show her you like her? Maybe put a frog in her shirt?"

"It's not like that. She's the Cyclops to my Wolverine." I don't believe a single word I'm saying, and he knows it.

"Right. Sure. Of the two of you, you're definitely the one with the claws," he says with a patronizing nod.

"Shut up and put the game in, would you?" I hand him the Madden cartridge after I finally find it in the Halo case, then I busy myself returning the rest of the games to their rightful homes.

He switches the inputs on the TV and begins to set everything up. "Do you want to know what I think?" he asks, clicking through the initial screens.

"Not really, but I'm sure you're gonna tell me anyway."

"I think you're full of it, and you like her. A lot."

I grunt and make a face, but I don't try to deny it this time.

Hearing Jordan call me out is concerning because it means I'm not hiding those thoughts from our friends as well as I should be. Jordan's not wrong. I do like her. But how I feel doesn't really matter if she's not into it.

"Whatever, man. It's not happening. We'd kill each other." I shrug.

I thought maybe Alice was catching feelings for me too, but when I tried to kiss her the other night, her body went rigid and she wouldn't talk. It was like she completely froze. Maybe our kiss at the wedding was just a fluke. Maybe she's upset about her dad. Or maybe she's just as confused as I am. But what I know for sure is that she doesn't want to be in a relationship with me. She said so like a hundred times. I can't go falling for Alice Caulfield.

"Earth to Roomie." Jordan waves his controller from the couch. "We doin' this or what?"

I nod and park myself next to him.

I manage to get in two good rounds before Jordan completely hands me my ass. Then I need to head out. The appointments I scheduled are today.

When I roll up to the house, Mr. Caulfield is already waiting on the porch. I still can't believe he actually took me up on the offer to drive him.

"Hi, Mr. Caulfield. How are you doing today?"

The grunt he gives me as he climbs into my passenger seat tells me this is likely to be a long ride with a lot of one-sided conversation.

"I'm glad you called," I try again. "I decided to schedule a session for myself, too. Couldn't hurt, right?"

The hour-long drive is tense and filled with nothing but more grunts and shrugs from my reluctant passenger as I try to engage with him until we finally arrive at the office building. After we check in, a guy who doesn't look much older than me comes up and introduces himself to Earl. They shake hands and disappear down the hall. I spend a few more minutes flipping through magazines in the waiting room until they call me back. I'm nervous, but sort of relieved that chauffeuring Alice's dad gives me an excuse to be here.

Eventually, a woman my mom's age greets me, her dark hair pulled back in a clip that reminds me of a claw machine.

"Hello, Jacob. I'm Monica. Nice to meet you."

"Hi. You can call me Jake."

"This way, please." She leads me into her office and gestures toward the couch.

"Should I lie down or something?"

She sets herself in the plaid armchair a few feet away. "You can, if you'd like. Or you can also just take a seat. Whatever makes you the most comfortable." Monica's voice is soft.

"Sorry. I don't really know how this is supposed to work." I sit and fold my hands on my lap, then unfold them immediately because I'm worried it makes my body language seem closed-off, and maybe she's judging me for that. My knees bounce and suddenly my mouth is dry.

"There's no agenda. This is your time. Today is only about getting to know you and what you'd like to get out of our next few sessions together. I have all of the forms you submitted in your intake, but I'd like to hear from you why you're here."

If I knew what my goals were, I wouldn't need to be here. "I don't know how to answer that."

"That's perfectly fine. Why don't you tell me a little bit about yourself to start?"

"Okay. I'm Jake. I live in North Bay. I was going to school for graphic design, but I dropped out last year. I only had one year left of college, but I just couldn't force myself through it. After that, I've been having some problems with my parents, friends, and my job...or lack thereof. Oh, and I have a dog. Her name's Hazel, and she's getting really old. I'm a little worried about losing her soon." I pause, and Monica looks at me like she's waiting for me to go on. "I was at a bachelor party recently, and therapy came up. Then my friend's dad needed a ride to an appointment here, and it sort of felt like a sign that I should try this."

"Had you ever thought about therapy before that?"

"Yeah, but it's not really encouraged in my house. My parents think it's a waste of time and money. They think it's pointless and lazy to pay someone to sit and listen to you complain. No offense."

Monica smiles politely, but I hope I haven't hurt her feelings.

"They have a lot of strong opinions I don't agree with. I feel like I'm rambling. Was that an okay answer? I'm not sure I'm doing this right."

"There are no right or wrong answers right now. Is that something you think about often? Whether you are doing things correctly?"

"Well, yeah. Doesn't everyone?"

"Some more so than others. Is there something in particular you're worried about today, or something you were hoping to talk about?"

"I don't know. I mean, yeah, there's a lot of stuff on my mind but…" I shrug and fix my eyes on a landscape print on the opposite wall. It's all so embarrassing to say out loud, especially when I know there are much bigger problems in the world. Am I really about to sit here and tell this woman I'm a poor little rich boy who got the sads because my mommy and daddy didn't pat me on the head enough times while I tried to show off for them? There are people starving, for chrissake. Earl is right down the hall working through the scars from a literal war. "I feel like such a jackass right now." I tug on the back of my neck. But if I'm going to do this for real, I have to be honest. So, I take a breath and force myself to look at her. "There's a lot of disapproval in my house, I guess."

"Disapproval? Can you tell me more about that?"

"Uh. I think, well, I *know* my parents had a different path in mind for me, and the way I'm living my life right now doesn't meet their expectations."

"I see. You seem upset by that. Do you find it feels heavy to carry the weight of other people's concerns?"

I blink at her. I never thought about it like that, but yeah, it's heavy.

"Everybody thinks I'm supposed to be perfect all the time. It's always been that way. Once I got a ninety-three on a fourth-grade math test, and I still remember my dad's face when he asked me what happened. He made me redo every single one of the problems, even the ones I got right, then he drove me to school early the next day so I could hand them to my teacher and apologize for not studying harder or paying enough attention in her class. So, yeah. It can be intense."

"That sounds like a lot of pressure. You say you don't want to follow your parents' plan for your life. Do you have a different path in mind for yourself?"

"I don't really know."

"Can I tell you a secret?" She leans back and smiles. "Most people are just winging it. It's okay if the answer is no and you don't have a plan."

"My dad's response to that would be that I'm supposed to be better than most people."

"Hmm. Is that also how you feel?"

"It's definitely not how I want to feel, but I don't know how to get that nagging voice out of my head. I guess that's why I'm here." If I didn't feel the need to meet those high expectations every time, life would be a lot less stressful.

A soft beep comes from her watch to let us know time is up for today.

"Well, that's our time. This was a good first session, Jake. Would you like to schedule again in two weeks?"

"Sure, thanks."

When I walk back to the lobby, Mr. Caulfield is standing by the water cooler. He tips his paper cup at me and knocks it back like he's taking a shot of something stronger.

"You really think rehashing all that old shit is gonna mean something to Alice?" he asks, eyes scanning me from head to toe.

I nod at him. "I do."

He nods back at me, just once, firmly. "Guess we better book the next one then." He shuffles over to the desk to grumble at the receptionist.

Therapy isn't what I expected it to be. Not that I thought I would spend one hour on a couch and suddenly be a different person. It's just that Monica and I didn't really accomplish anything today. Or maybe we did, but I can't identify what it is. I still don't know if I'm doing it right. But maybe the point is learning to be okay with that.

Chapter 26

Jake

I stop outside of The Blue Crab and stare at the building across the street. Kyle took down the Get the Scoop sign yesterday. His retirement marks the end of an era, but it also presents a rare opportunity. There's real estate available on Main Street. And there's hardly any competition for it, thanks to the water damage caused by a malfunctioning sump pump that couldn't handle our last storm. The building will need major renovations, and so far, no one else seems up to the challenge. I'm not afraid to put in some elbow grease. But if I'm going to act on this crazy idea, I know I can't do it alone.

I turn and enter the restaurant. I texted Alice earlier and asked her to meet me here for lunch. She thinks I want to talk about my art classes. Technically, I do, but now it's going to involve a lot more than volunteering once a week at the library.

I find a seat and put in an order for a large plate of seasoned Old Bay fries and two sodas, and Ms. Edna brings everything out quickly. I look up when Alice plops down across from me in the booth. She picks up a handful of fries and pops them into her mouth.

"What's up? You wanted to talk to me?" she says through a mouthful.

"I do. Remember how I talked about starting a community art studio one day?"

She nods.

I point to the window, and she turns her head to look at the old Victorian-style building across the street. "What if I said I want to do it now? Would you be in?"

"I'm not following."

"Look, I'll be honest. It's going to be a ton of work to get this off the ground, and I'm not expecting to turn huge profits. But I want to make this happen, and I need help. I need someone who loves art and this town as much as I do. You're the only person in North Bay who meets that description. I put in an offer on Kyle's building. Are you interested in being my business partner?"

She blinks at me. "I mean, I do think it's an amazing idea," Alice says, cautiously. "I would love to start an indie imprint and work at a studio. Maybe host some writing groups. But your uncle is an actual real estate developer. Why aren't you asking him? I don't know the first thing about running a business."

"Sure, you do. You're already selling your books online. You're way ahead of me. You're an established working artist."

"This is totally different, and you know it. Where would we get the money for an entire building, Jake? The down payment alone has to be like..." She shakes her head. "A lot."

I force myself to hold eye contact, but I don't want to say the words because I know she'll freak out.

She stares back at me. "Why aren't you worried about the money, Jake? Ugh. Do you have an actual trust fund? Like in the movies? Oh, God. You do, don't you?"

Guilty. I don't say anything, but she takes my silence as confirmation.

Alice whines, "I didn't know you were *that* kind of rich. A trust fund? That's like *Thank you Jeeves, but we don't need to book a ski vacation in the Alps, we'll be summering in Nantucket* sort of money. You're sitting here acting like you need my input, but I can't function on the same level as someone who summers as a verb, Jake."

Called it. I knew she'd freak out.

"It's not that serious. It's literally just a different kind of bank account. What am I supposed to do? Ignore the inheritance my grandparents chose to leave me? Wouldn't that be kind of rude, if you think about it? Besides, you know we do our summering in the south of France." I wink at her, trying to lighten the tension.

She groans, but to her credit, she shakes it off. "If we're doing this, I'm not riding your coattails. If I'm getting involved, I want to be an actual investor. I won't be able to contribute much, but I want to buy in for at least five percent ownership."

"Fine. That's fair."

She leans across the table to whisper, "Did you really summer in France?"

I laugh. "No. Do you not remember seeing me right here every summer of your life? I've never been to France. My parents have. I, on the other hand, am not even a hundred percent sure I know where Nantucket is, if I'm being honest." I can't think straight around Alice these days. I feel like there's a fifty-fifty chance it's a fictional place and I'm making an ass out of myself.

She sighs. "It's an island in Massachusetts."

"See? This is exactly why I need you. We could be a good team. Please, Alice. Say yes." I stick out my lower lip and bat my eye lashes.

"Ugh. Don't go all puppy dog on me. It's actually a pretty cool idea." I knew she'd see it. "What would you call it?"

"I don't know. I don't really want it to be something cheesy like Brew-Ha-Ha or Get the Scoop. For me, it's not about the marketing and branding. I get that we have to do that part. But I hate the idea of commercializing it too much. I wish the focus could just stay on the art."

"There you go, that's the name then." She smiles.

"What?" I didn't suggest anything.

"Just Art."

I take a minute to roll it over. "I like it."

She takes another sip of her soda, and there's a long pause before she says, "Okay, I'm in. But I have one rule. "

"Name it."

"We're officially working together now, we don't want things to get messy. We're colleagues, and we're friends. That's it. It has to stay that way. No more hookups. Sex is off the table."

I shrug. "I mean, we never did it on the table anyway, so..."

"Jake!" She blushes, and I laugh while I clink my glass to hers and tip it back, hoping she doesn't notice I didn't actually agree to that.

Chapter 27

Alice

"This place is going to look amazing when you two are done with it." Danielle says as she hip-checks the door of the former Get the Scoop ice cream shop and pushes it open with her foot. She's holding a cardboard drink carrier filled with three Brew-Ha-Ha to-go cups. "One latte with oat milk," she says, joining us at the table and putting a cup down in front of me. "One regular coffee with three sugars." She hands Jake one, too. Then she sits down next to him with her own cup of chai.

Today came more quickly than expected, but Jake is Jake, and he didn't waste any time buying the ice cream shop as soon as Kyle put it up for sale. Now that it's official and we've made some progress on renovations, we invited Danielle to stop by and see it.

"Thanks for bringing these." I turn the cup slowly in my hands. Our best friend knows our drink orders by heart. I hate that she doesn't know everything.

Jake runs a hand over the two-day-old stubble on his face and leans forward, putting his elbows on the table. He doesn't like this either. We've never lied to Danielle before, and we both agree we need to come clean.

"What's this uncomfortable vibe I'm sensing? Oh no. Did I catch you two in the middle of another fight? What is it this time?" she asks, sounding half-amused, half-exhausted with us.

"The opposite, actually," Jake says.

"We aren't fighting," I say at the same time.

She looks at me quizzically, then shifts to face him. "You're both being weird. Just tell me. What's this about?"

There's a long pause before Jake reaches across the table and places his hand on top of mine. Danielle's eyes follow the movement, then come up to meet my face. I nod at both of them. It's time.

Jake starts to explain, "Alice and I—"

"We had sex." I cut him off.

Jake closes his eyes and sighs. We talked about this. He was hoping for a more tactful approach, but I think it's better to just rip off the Band-aid. For the briefest moment Danielle flinches and looks stricken, like I've slapped her, but she quickly plasters a smile back on her face.

"Oh. Um. Okay. I'm not sure what to say to that. Congratulations, I guess? You're both adults. Good for you. Thanks for telling me, but you didn't need to." Her voice falters. "When?" she asks. "No, never mind. Don't feel like you need to answer that."

"The night of the hurricane," I say.

"Before the wedding? So, when we were cleaning out your dad's place, you two were already—"

"Dan-Dan," Jake interrupts her but doesn't say anything more. He clearly doesn't want to be having this conversation in this much detail.

"No. Um. It's fine. You don't need my permission. I'm a little surprised is all." She takes a sip and swallows, then she chews on her lip. "Wow. Okay. So are you two are, like, a thing? I have to say, I did not see this coming."

The way Jake's shy smile comes across the table just for me is a sharp contrast to the unease pooling in my belly as I watch my best friend stumble through our news.

"No. We're not. And we're not going to be," I tell her honestly, and I watch as Jake's mouth falls. "We just didn't like keeping a secret from you."

"Right. Sure. That makes sense. Well, the place is looking great. I'm really happy for you both, but I told Edna I would stop by The Blue Crab today, so I better head over there." Danielle stands and offers us a small wave before excusing herself in a hurry.

"That could have gone better," Jake says when the door closes.

I hide behind my latte and try not to resent our mutual best friend because she has confirmed what I already knew: there is no way being anything besides Jake's business partner can work. We don't make sense. If not even Danielle can get on board, then no one else in our lives will support it. We'll alienate everyone while we simultaneously run this brand-new business into the ground. And for what? Maybe a few weeks of hot sex and a doomed relationship that will fizzle out the second we come back to our senses and remember how much we've never been able to stand each other?

Jake and I sit together for a few minutes, and neither of us says a word until I finally tell him I'm going to find Danielle and talk to our friend. Alone.

He gives me a stiff nod, and I walk outside.

It doesn't take long to spot her across the street outside The Blue Crab. She's sitting on the wooden glider that overlooks the water. She sees me and motions for me to join her. I do, although now my mind is stuck back in the studio, picturing the way Jake looked so hurt when I denied there was more between us. We're both quiet, watching our feet swing.

"Seems like someone is lost in thought," she observes.

"Hm? Oh, yeah. I guess."

"Those thoughts wouldn't happen to be about a tall, dark, and handsome guy covered in bookish tattoos, would they?"

I hang my head and groan.

"Oh, I totally get the appeal," she says. "Welcome to your Main Character Era, babe. He wants you. It's so obvious. I think he probably always has in some capacity, and I was just too selfish to realize it."

"Hey. Don't talk about my best friend that way." I nudge her shoulder. "There's no way you could have known. Jake and I didn't even know. I still can't wrap my brain around it. But just to clarify, yes, we did have sex, but we still aren't together."

"Maybe not yet. But I could see it." She gives me a small smile. "Sorry I bailed. I just needed a minute to process. It took me by surprise."

"Believe me, you weren't the only one."

Danielle laughs. "I mean, it's a *big* surprise. My mind is pretty blown right now. I'm flabbergasted. Truly. All my flabbers have been gasted. I had a feeling you two might like each other because you seemed to be getting along so well, but I had no idea you were already hooking up. I can't believe I didn't figure it out. I guess it just never seemed like a possibility in my mind."

I let out a small, relieved laugh. If she's joking, she must not be too angry. "Right? Are we seriously sitting here talking about me and *Jake?* But don't worry. It was just an extended hookup. Nothing more. And it's over."

"Hmm." She studies my face. "It caught me off guard, I admit, but I actually think you two make a lot of sense together. You have so much in common."

Now I'm the flabbergasted one. Has she lost her mind? "Jake and I couldn't be more different. We can't even agree about pizza toppings," I huff.

"I'm talking about the important stuff. You're both artists. You both like those crazy pranks. You've both been amazing friends to me for our whole lives." She ticks off a list on her fingers. "Plus, you're both passionate and stubborn. And finally, you and Jake are both lucky to have me to set you straight in times such as these, because neither one of you thinks you deserve to be happy. But you do. You both do. And I am more than willing to stick my nose in and nudge you along until you figure that out for yourselves."

"Even if that stuff were true, it's still not smart to get involved in a relationship with my business partner," I protest.

She stares me down. "Do you remember last year right before I started dating Mike? You sat me down for some hard truths over our morning lattes."

I hesitate before admitting, "Yeah…"

"Well, buckle up, Buttercup. The shoe is on the other foot, and I'm about to tell you something that's gonna be hard to hear."

I let out a long breath, then motion for her to lay it on me. "I think I can take it."

"You, Alice Caulfield, are a scaredy cat. You're afraid to admit you want to be with Jake because it means admitting you were wrong about him. And you're also scared because it means everything will be different. I know things will change between all of us, but that's part of growing up. Change is going to happen anyway, and if things are going to be shaken up regardless, I'd rather see you both happy on the other side of it."

"That's a pretty good point."

"I'm not finished. You're also terrified because you know Jake can go toe-to-toe with you, and you won't be able to bulldoze him. He challenges you, and you do the same thing for him. Neither of you is used to being confronted like that. But you both need it."

I groan and hide my face in my hands, resting my elbows on my lap while we glide. I think she might be right. I am scared. But it's more than that. "He's done so much for me lately between starting the business and helping with my dad. The only thing I have to offer him in return is…me. It's not an even trade. It's not fair to ask it of him," I admit.

"Why don't you get back in there and let him make that decision for himself?"

Chapter 28

Jake

I don't know what Danielle said to her, but it seems like Alice came back to the studio extra feisty and looking for a fight. She's throwing out reasons why we can't be together. It's a long list, but nothing new. I've heard them all from her before, but something about this time is different. I swear she wants me to argue. This doesn't feel like all the times she wished I would shut my mouth and leave her alone. If I didn't know better, I'd think she wants me to tell her she's wrong and we should go for it. But she's made it perfectly clear that's not what she wants from me. So far, I've managed to stay calm and let her vent her frustration, but my patience is hanging by the thinnest thread.

"Seriously, Jake, we can't be more than business partners. It would be a disaster."

"I know, Ace. You've said as much, and I don't recall asking for more from you."

"It could mess up your whole dream for this place. Besides, we're from two different worlds. I don't even know how to play golf!" she yells.

Golf?

I don't know why that's what finally makes the dam break, but this time I yell right back at her. "Do I strike you as the kind of guy who wants to book a tee time and run over to the country club? Do you think I'm standing around, creaming my khakis at the thought of brunch on Sundays?"

"Oh, come on. Who doesn't like brunch? Everyone loves brunch." She can't stop herself from contradicting every word out of my mouth.

This might be the stupidest argument we've ever had. I don't even know what a person who doesn't eat meat or dairy could have at a brunch. Oatmeal? There's no way she actually feels this passionately about oatmeal. She just has to fight, because that's what we bring out of each other. I understand, because I feel the same frustration pulsing through me.

I step forward, and she does the same until our bodies are only inches apart, and she points one finger into my chest. I want to grab her and throw her against the wall, stick my tongue in that loud mouth to make her stop talking. Although, knowing Alice, she'd probably bite it. Maybe I shouldn't find that hot, but I do.

Her phone buzzes in her pocket, and a little bit of the fire leaves her body. We both know she has to check the message. It could be about her dad. She sighs and pulls it out. Immediately, her shoulders relax, and I think I see a flash of humor in her eyes.

"Everything okay?" I know she wants to fight, and if that's what she needs from me I'm more than happy to oblige, but I still feel the need to make sure there isn't another emergency. As much as she drives me insane, I want her to be okay.

"It was nothing, not that it's any of your business."

As she lowers her phone, I catch a glimpse of the screen. It's an image of a prairie dog. I laugh, unable to help it, and she narrows her eyes at me.

"What?"

"I completely forgot I did that," I say, pointing at her phone.

She gasps. "Fuzzy Alice was from you?" The hard lines that etched her features seconds ago have softened.

"I thought naming a rodent after you would be a solid prank." I shrug. "But judging from the look on your face, it didn't annoy you as much as I thought it would."

She actually stomps her foot and crosses her arms, letting out a loud groan of frustration. "I hate when you make it impossible for me to hate you."

I smirk at that, and she points at my mouth.

"See? That's exactly what I'm talking about. I should hate your smug face."

"But you don't, do you?"

"But I don't. I really don't. And it's becoming a problem." She sighs a long, heavy breath.

I can relate. I don't hate her either. I never have.

Her voice is small when she launches into her explanation. "I wasn't allowed to have a pet growing up. I used to beg for a hamster because they were cute and pretty inexpensive, as far as pets go. But my parents always said no. Getting those pictures feels…it's almost like gaining back a piece of my childhood. It sounds stupid, but sometimes it's the best part of my week."

Whatever fight I had left in me evaporates. "That's not stupid at all."

I did that for her. Even though it wasn't intentional, knowing I made her feel that way warms me from the inside like a shot of good whiskey.

"But it sucks to find out I only have her because you were trying to be mean."

"I wasn't trying to be mean, I was trying to be annoying. You know, like glitter in a sock drawer or switching all the cases in someone's video game collection." I duck down to look at her face-to-face.

She's biting her lip, trying to hide the smile that wants to break through.

"Alice?"

She heaves another big sigh. "What?"

"I think we should go on a real date."

Chapter 29

Alice

Jake and I are on his uncle's boat, gliding across the bay on our first official date. Hazel is lying at his feet, basking in the sun. The wind is doing crazy things to my hair, and I wish I'd thought to wear a hat. I know Jake will give me his if I ask, but then I wouldn't have this view of him in a backward cap, with the veins on his arms popping as he stands and grips the steering wheel.

"Do you want to drive?" Jake asks over the hum of the engine.

"Can't. Don't have a boating license." I shrug.

Jake turns his head to blink at me slowly. "How is that possible? You've lived in North Bay as long as I have."

"Not all of us grew up with our own boat in the backyard," I remind him. "What was I going to do with a boating license?"

"Drive a boat," he says matter-of-factly. "That's usually what people do with it."

"Like I said, can't."

Jake keeps one hand on the wheel and angles the rest of his body to face me. Hazel lifts her head to watch us, but immediately gets bored and sets it down again.

"Come here." He's smiling and being all encouraging when he motions to the space between his body and the steering wheel. There's not much extra room there because the raised captain's chair is behind him, and a certain lazy dog is only inches away.

I smirk. "Nah. Danielle can teach me."

"How do you think she learned? I won't let you crash us," he promises.

I let out a small huff, but I walk over and squeeze my body in front of his, and my arm grazes the billowing fabric of his T-shirt. The sleeves are cut off, putting both of his tatted biceps on full display as he puts his hands on my hips. He smells like sunscreen and just a hint of cologne.

"If I'd known nobody else was teaching you, I would have done this a long time ago." Jake reaches past my shoulder to adjust the gear shift and bring the boat to a slower speed.

"Wasn't your job."

"It is now." He bends so his face is closer to mine, and he lifts his sunglasses so he can look directly into my eyes. "Hands on the wheel. You'll do great." He kisses my forehead. "All right. I'm going to shut off the motor, and we'll start from the beginning. You already know how to drive a car, so it's going to be simple. This is basically the same, but easier. No pedals and less traffic. Docking can be tricky, but we'll save that for another day."

My chest squeezes at the idea of another date. "I just turn the key?"

Jake moves his mouth closer to my ear. I feel the warmth of his breath on my neck, and it gives me goosebumps I'm grateful to be able to blame on the cool wind. He continues with the lesson. "On this kind of boat, yes. On the smaller ones, like the aluminum jon boat we take out fishing, you steer the motor with a stick. I'll show you that, too. But for now, go ahead and start the ignition."

I turn the key, and the motor kicks on again. Jake briefly explains what each of the markings on the dash does, then he points to a buoy in the distance.

He puts a hand on my shoulder and squeezes lightly. "Head in that direction. You've got this."

Then he steps back and watches as I drive the boat a few hundred feet in a straight line.

When we approach the buoy, I let out a yell. "I did it!"

Jake laughs. "I saw."

Without thinking, I close the few steps of distance between us and throw my arms around him. He chuckles as he hugs me back, but at the same time, he maneuvers our bodies so he can regain control of the boat before it runs directly into the channel marker.

"Oops." I unhook my arms. Immediately, they feel empty.

"All good. You did a great job. Next time maybe just make sure nothing's in the path of collision before you abandon your post. Otherwise, no notes."

"Fair. I can do that." I smile.

He nods. "Of course you can. Now I have a very important question. Think hard before you answer. Ready?"

"Hit me."

"Do you want to eat lunch here on the boat, or do you want to go over to the beach?"

"The beach" is what locals call the small island in the middle of the bay. It's not big enough for any homes or utilities, but boaters pull up and use the sandy area on its shore for recreation. Teenagers go there to hang out with friends, throw Frisbees, or sneak beers. It's also a popular make-out destination.

"Let's check out the beach."

"Done."

It only takes a few minutes before we're pulling up to the shore and Jake beaches the boat. He lowers Hazel down onto the sand and grabs a backpack from a side compartment. Then he hops out into the shallow water and extends his arms to help me down. I'm spending a lot of time in these arms today, and I have no complaints.

Hazel follows as we walk along the beach until Jake stops and sets the backpack on the sand. He unzips it and pulls out a striped, oversized beach towel, which he spreads out for us to use as a picnic blanket.

"I figured peanut butter and jelly should be safe enough. No meat, no dairy, right?" he says as he pulls two metal water bottles and some sandwiches from the pack.

I beam at him as I sit down on the blanket. "Thank you. I love PB and J. And I was surprised to learn recently that peanut butter is considered a liquid. Did you know that?"

Jake chuckles and sits next to me. "You don't say."

He takes out a collapsible bowl and pours water into it, holding it out for Hazel. She dives in sloppily before returning to her favorite spot at Jake's feet. We eat our sandwiches, then we lie on the towel, shoulders touching while we listen to the water lap onto the shore.

"You know, Ace, it's almost August. We're going to have to think of a creative way to celebrate your birthday."

"Oh yeah? This oughta be good."

"I'll think of something."

I roll onto my side to face him, and he does the same. We stay quiet and still, concentrating on each other while everything else around us seems to fade away. Eventually, I can't take it anymore.

"The way you're looking at me right now makes me want to kiss you," I repeat the line he used on me our first night at the cottage, and from the way his lips part and eyes darken, it seems to work just as well on him.

"I think I want that, too." He remembers what I said in return.

I think I might actually be falling for Jacob Freaking Gibson.

I grab the front of his shirt and pull him toward me. He tastes like peanut butter and salt, and with his lips on mine, I hardly notice the sand in my hair or the water breaking onto the shore just beneath our feet.

Chapter 30

Alice

"Dress looks nice." My dad nods at me. He's having a good day today.

"Thanks." I fidget with the bangle bracelet on my wrist and straighten my skirt.

From far away, the pattern on this maxi dress looks floral, but when you get up close you realize the pictures are tiny dinosaurs with different kinds of plants in their mouths. I have no clue where we're going, but this is the kind of fun summer dress that seems like it could work for lots of occasions.

Jake wants to take me out to celebrate my birthday, which is coming up at the end of this month, and to thank me for helping with his art classes. I told him creating the art for my book was more than enough, but he waved that idea away. He's kept our destination a surprise so far, but I'll find out soon enough because he's due to pick me up any minute.

My chest feels tight when I hear the knock on our front door, but as soon as I open it, some of the tightness melts away. He's wearing a white linen button-down and navy pants. When my gaze finally travels up to his smile, I realize I've been staring for longer than necessary.

"Hi."

"Hey."

"Do you think this outfit will work?" I motion to my dress. "I figured it should be good as long as we aren't planning to go hiking in the woods or something. Right?"

"You look great, Alice," he reassures me, tucking a strand of hair behind my ear.

My dad comes to the door to say hi and shake Jake's hand.

"Good to see you, sir," Jake tells him. Then he turns to me. "I'm excited for you to see what we're doing. I hope you like it."

"Can I have a hint? The suspense is making me nervous."

"Sure," he leads me down to his car and opens the door for me to get inside. Once he buckles himself into the driver's seat, he turns to face me before starting the engine. "I want to be clear, you can always say no. But have you ever heard of boudoir photos?"

The tightness returns. "First, that's not how hints work. Second, we've been dating for less than three weeks, and you made an appointment for a stranger to take pictures of me in my underwear?" I'm not even wearing a bra with this dress.

"Technically, I made an appointment for a stranger to take pictures of *us*. I booked a couple's shoot because I didn't want you to feel like you had to do it alone. Which, now that I'm saying it out loud, I realize may have been a step too far. If you think you'd rather do it by yourself, that's cool, too. Or you don't have to do it at all. No pressure. This is supposed to be about you."

I feel my forehead crease as I scrunch my face at him.

He lowers his eyes for a second before they meet mine again. "I've been thinking about it a lot, and I hate that you have any bad memories associated with pictures of your body." He takes my hand and gives it a gentle squeeze. "I want you to be able to see yourself the same way I see you. I thought maybe we could replace some of those old memories with new ones and show you exactly how beautiful you are." His voice is tender. He moves his seatbelt out of the way and leans over to kiss my cheek. It's sweet, and gentle, and over way too soon.

"I'm still not sure I'm dressed for this." I shift my own seatbelt back into place, the tightness in my chest easing again.

"Don't worry. I'm told there are a lot of wardrobe options. Let's go and see how you feel. If you decide you're uncomfortable, we leave immediately. No questions asked. I won't fight you. You're in charge today. Deal?" He glances over at me, looking tentative.

I nod. "Okay." I can see why he didn't tell me about this. I definitely would've freaked out for days and ultimately chickened out. But I can already picture a series of black-and-white photos of a shirtless Jake wearing ripped jeans and staring pensively out a window. I don't have any idea what kind of magic tricks a photographer would have to do to make me look as good next to him, but I'm intrigued enough to at least scope it out.

We drive through North Bay, out into Marnock, and a little beyond until we reach a warehouse with only one other car parked outside.

"You're sure you spoke with a real photographer, right? Because this is sketchy as hell."

Jake laughs. "Yes. It's legit, I promise." He parks the car and turns to face me fully, then his voice is serious as he assures me again,

"I have no expectations here. You don't have to do anything you don't want to do. I really do just want you to be able to see yourself the way you deserve to be seen."

I sigh. "This is actually really thoughtful, and I think I want to do it, assuming we don't get murdered in the next ten minutes. But I am nervous. What if these pictures look like trash? I'm sure you paid a lot of money for this. I'm not a model."

"Listen. I'm taking off my friend and business partner hat and putting on my boyfriend hat, so don't hold any of what I'm about to say against me in the studio."

My heart dances. "Boyfriend, huh?" I beam at him.

He smiles back. "You heard me. And as your boyfriend, I'm telling you you're gorgeous and sexy and feminine, and right now my biggest concern is not if these pictures will turn out well. I know they'll be hot no matter what, because you're in them. But I am a little worried because I don't know how I'm supposed to contain my *excitement* the entire time." He looks down at his lap.

I roll my eyes. "Must be nice to live a life where your biggest concern about entering an abandoned warehouse is how much attention will be focused on your pants." I smirk and pat his cheek. "I'm sure they'll give you a pillow to hold or something. You got us into this, and you're not getting out of it."

He turns his face to plant a kiss on my palm.

When we step into the warehouse a woman wearing dark wash jeans and a linen shirt greets us. Her long curls hang down over her shoulders.

"Hi, I'm Elliotte Shawn. You must be Alice. Welcome to the studio. I'm excited to do your shoot today, if you decide you're ready.

I don't want you to feel any pressure. When I spoke to your partner, I told him I don't typically recommend surprising someone with this experience."

"He warned me before we got here. It was a little bit of a shock, but I actually think I might be excited. But fair warning, I've never done this before. I don't know what I'm doing, and I think I wore the wrong underwear."

She has a friendly laugh. "That's okay. I have an entire wardrobe selection. We can do anything from full coverage in the clothes you're wearing to the lingerie we provide. Or fully nude. Anything you choose from our costume department is professionally cleaned after every client. It's entirely up to you and your comfort level. And if at any point you change your mind about a decision, just let me know. We can stop and regroup."

"Can you walk me through the process a little bit? I'm sort of nervous," I admit.

"Nerves are totally normal. It's my job to help you feel as beautiful and comfortable as possible. Today is all about celebrating your body. We start with hair and makeup, then pick out what you'd like to wear. After that, we'll spend some time taking pictures in different poses with some of the various props around the studio."

Jake hangs back to give us some privacy while Elliotte walks me through the warehouse and shows me where sections are curtained off and staged to look like rooms. There's a four-poster bed behind the first curtain, a wooden swing behind the second, and finally, a large tufted ottoman behind the third. A separate area is more industrial, with a brick wall and concrete floor.

"All of these options for the background and props are available to you. I keep a closed set. When it's time to take the photos, we send hair and makeup home and it will only be you, your partner, me, and my assistant. Her job is to be here as another advocate for your safety and comfort as well as to help me set up the equipment and demonstrate the poses."

Next, we go to another area sectioned off by a wall of velvet curtains, and Elliotte explains that we'll look through some of the outfit choices and decide what best fits my style. That way the hair and makeup team will know which direction to go.

"So, the vibe I'm getting from your dino dress and the way you styled your hair today is fun and playful. I love the lavender." She points to the top of my head. "We can definitely lean into that, or there are a few other ways we could take it."

"What about an Old Hollywood theme?" I suggest. "With lots of black and white and, like, timeless fabrics."

"Love it. That's one of our most popular choices, actually. I have some sample shots I can show you. Velvet and lace can lend a classic, sensual feeling to your shoot."

"Perfect."

As Elliotte walks away to grab the examples, Jake comes up to me. His expression is neutral.

"Was this too much, too soon?" he asks. "I'm realizing I sort of assumed you'd be down for this, and I didn't mean to steamroll you into it."

"You didn't. Elliotte seems great. I think we even landed on a theme. How do you feel about putting on a tux?"

He laughs. "That sounds like a lot more clothing than I expected to be wearing. But like I told you, I'm fine with whatever you want to do while we're here." He moves to stand behind me and puts his arms around my waist.

"Oh, don't worry. I'm sure the tux will be coming off soon enough." I press my body into his and move my hips in a slow circle. "I'm already picturing photos of you taking off your tie and walking toward me while I pose on that big old bed for you."

He drops his voice and brushes his nose over my earlobe as he asks, "Yeah? And what will you be wearing?"

"You'll see soon enough," I tell him as the hair and makeup team arrives.

An hour and a half later, my short locks are framing my face in pin curls, and my lips are painted a deep, glossy red. My eyes are highlighted with dark colors and long false lashes. The team did a few touch-ups on Jake, too, so he won't be shiny in the photos. Elliotte dismisses the hair and makeup duo and introduces us to her assistant, Tasha, who is setting up the cameras around the tufted ottoman and draping sheer white fabric over the furniture.

"You look...wow." Jake shakes his head as if he's almost speechless when he sees me in the floor-length silk robe that offers full coverage but still makes me feel incredibly sexy. Underneath, I'm wearing a strappy blue lingerie set I love so much that I might have to order one for myself when we leave.

"I could say the same to you."

He looks practically edible in that tux with the tie hanging undone and the top two buttons on his shirt open.

"Here we go." He squeezes my hand and leads me onto the set.

"So, Alice will be here." Elliotte points to the ottoman and demonstrates how she wants me positioned. "And Jake, you'll stand behind her like this and slowly start to pull the robe off her shoulder. When he does that, Alice, I want you to look up at him and arch your back. I know these positions don't feel natural, but remember, the stranger it feels, the better it will look on camera."

"Okay. I think I've got this," Jake says.

I nod. "Let's try it."

As we pose and slowly run our hands along each other's shoulders, Elliotte and Tasha chirp encouragement. I feel his arms flex under my touch.

"You okay?" he asks, adjusting the robe so it covers more of my lower half.

I nod. "I really am."

"You're both doing great!" Elliotte beams. "Now, Jake, let's do pants but no shirt on you for the next shot. Go ahead and kneel on the floor in front of Alice. I want you to look up like you're worshiping her. Alice, spread your legs nice and wide so he can get as close to you as possible. Let the robe fall open. His head will block your chest from the camera for now."

Jake follows her instructions to the letter, but midway through shooting the pose, his hands slip into my robe to tickle me. I yelp and accidentally knee him in the chest, which sends him flying back onto the floor. Thankfully, he isn't hurt, and we both start laughing. Tasha and Elliotte think it's as funny as we do.

We're having so much fun it's hard to hold the poses because we all keep cracking up.

We manage to get through two more positions with the robe, then it's time to spotlight the strappy two-piece when we move over to the swing.

It's harder than I would have expected to reach up and grab the ropes on each side while I arch my back and cross my legs at the ankle. I'm earning a new respect for the models who pose like this every day. The muscles in my arms are straining while Jake stands aside for a few shots. Judging from the smoldering heat behind his eyes as he watches me, I'm starting to believe I might look as sexy as I feel.

Chapter 31

Jake

"Are we ready to move on to the next look?" Elliotte asks. Tasha adjusts a ring light and gives her a thumbs-up. "Jake, let's keep the trousers but no shirt for now, and you lie down on the bed. Alice, are you ready to remove the top?" When Alice nods at her, she continues. "Awesome. You're going to sit with your knees on either side of him. I'll drape the blankets strategically. You look down at Jake while he looks up at you." Elliotte repositions the sheets while she directs us. "This part might sound weird, but I need you looking at each other's chins, okay? It reads better in the final photos that way."

The camera clicks, and we try to hold still. This is somehow both the most erotic and most awkward hour of my life. Alice straddles me, topless, wearing only thin bikini bottoms, with two other women in the room. It sounds hot, and it definitely is, but mostly I'm trying to keep up with all the choreography they're throwing at me. Elliotte and Tasha are on the bed next to us, fully clothed while they demonstrate our next pose.

"So, Jake, if you're comfortable we'll go with just boxer briefs on you for the next few shots. You sit up against the headboard, and

Alice will turn her back to you. Alice, you sit over him, like this." Tasha places her knees on either side of Elliotte and arches her body, reaching behind her to cup the back of her boss's neck. Elliotte reaches across Tasha and shows me how one of my arms will be wrapped around Alice's chest to cover her, while my opposite hand will be splayed over her collarbone. My head should go into her neck.

I lose the pants and Alice climbs into her position. Tasha arranges the sheet, and the camera starts clicking once again.

My mouth is next to Alice's ear, so I take the opportunity to check in again. "How are you doing?" Her skin is warm and soft, and there is a thin layer of sweat beading between us under the heat of the lights. This has officially gone way beyond the realm of what could be considered normal for a brand-new relationship.

"I'm good, I promise," she assures me.

Elliotte suggests Alice turn to face me for the next pose, so we take a few shots with her riding my lap, holding tight to the headboard behind me. Then it's time for some additional shots of Alice by herself. For the final images, Tasha dusts Alice with some shimmering gold dust, and I swear she looks like an actual goddess, confident and strong and so goddamn beautiful I'm almost afraid to blink because how can this woman be real?

"Great job. I think that's a wrap," Elliotte says. "You can both get dressed and meet me over in my office. I'll show you a few of the raw shots before you leave. It will take me a few weeks to complete the final edits."

Alice hurries to put on her dress while I slip back into my own clothes. Once we're both presentable again, she finds me outside the dressing rooms.

"That was so much more fun than I thought it would be." She's glowing from more than just the gold dust. I don't know if I've ever seen her this happy.

"Yeah?" I smile at her. "So, you're not traumatized?" Honestly, it could've gone either way. It was a big risk, and I'm thrilled it paid off. She looks great, but more importantly, she seems proud of herself.

"It was a little weird at first, but you were right. Everyone was super kind and professional. I didn't feel cheap or sleazy at all."

I wince. I hate the implication those old pictures she took for Owen could have made her feel that way, but I fix my face quickly. "I'm sorry, can you repeat that? It sounded like you said 'Jake, you were right.'"

She laughs. "Well, that couldn't possibly be true now, could it?"

"Nah." I wink. Her cheeks look a bit flushed, but it could just be the makeup.

"All ready over here." Elliotte waves us over to her open office area and motions for us to sit in the chairs opposite the long metal table she uses as a desk. She clicks a few buttons on her laptop and turns the extra monitor to face us.

Alice gasps and her hand flies to her chest. I sit, blinking. I don't remember how to talk. There are no words for the image in front of us. I stare at our bodies, entwined and draped in fabric. The lighting is perfect, and the photo looks like it should be in a gallery. As she clicks through more of the images, Elliotte lands on one of Alice alone in the swing. It's a black-and-white picture that looks like it could be an album cover. Her head is back, and her arms are stretched high, gripping the ropes on either side. Her legs are crossed, and she's suspended in mid-air.

I need to swallow before I can speak. "These are great."

"Thank you. And you're happy, Alice?" Elliotte asks.

Beside me, Alice sits, staring. She seems transfixed by the screen. "So happy. I can't believe you made me look like this."

Elliotte laughs and taps the glass with a fingernail. "Unedited images, remember? This is all you. I'm glad you like them. It was a beautiful shoot."

No kidding. I may need to find a way to break the laws of physics on the way home, because there's no way I can get Alice home fast enough. I need to feel her gorgeous body on mine again.

Chapter 32

Alice

For my entire life I've heard things like "real women have curves," and I've always agreed that curvy women are beautiful, but the concept left me feeling inadequate. Staring at the raw footage of the photos on Elliotte's computer feels like peeking through a window into a parallel universe, one where I might be just as beautiful. The woman in these pictures doesn't seem small, or bony, or flat. The only thing that comes to mind is she looks…hot. Really hot. And she's me.

"No way," Jake tries to protest when he sees me reaching for my wallet. "This is supposed to be a gift."

As much as I appreciate what he's done by setting all of this up, he was right when he said this is something I need to do for myself.

"Listen, I will never be able to thank you enough for the idea, and I love that you're here, but I have to do this part on my own. I don't want to feel like I needed another man to buy my freedom from Owen." I'm not trying to diminish his gift, but if today is about taking my power back, then I need to know I did all of this with my own strength, and I want to own these photos in every possible way.

"I think I get what you're saying, so I'm not going to fight you on this, but you do realize now this means I need to come up with a whole new birthday gift, right?"

"Don't you dare. This was perfect."

I hand Elliotte my debit card while I scoot my chair closer to Jake so I can tuck my arm behind his back. When I lean into his side, his fingers reach up to brush the tiny hairs at the base of my neck. His touch sends goosebumps up my arms again, and a warm shiver runs through me. Elliotte thanks us and says she'll send a link to the digital files when they are ready.

We head back to Jake's apartment, and when we get inside, he takes two small ice cream cups from the freezer. They're like the ones our school used to sell in the cafeteria, but these are labeled dairy-free.

"We can't celebrate your birthday without these. It's tradition."

I shake my head and smile as he produces two tiny wooden spoons. "It's not even my birthday yet. But I suppose this is a gift I can accept. I haven't seen one of these since we were kids."

He peels the cardboard lid from his cup and leans a hip against the counter. "You know, I was trying to remember, and I can't think of a time I was ever invited to a birthday party for you while we were growing up."

"That's because I didn't have them," I tell him, stabbing the little spoon into the too-hard dessert.

"I was afraid that was going to be the reason. I almost hoped it was because you weren't a big fan of mine."

"What are you talking about? You and I were tight back then. Just maybe not as tight as my parents' budget." I shrug. "I definitely would've invited you if I had a party. You let me tag along that time your mom rented a bus to drive out to the arcade for your birthday."

"I remember that. Two kids puked up pizza and cake on the way home, and my mom complained for six months because she had to pay an extra cleaning fee." Jake shakes his head and smiles. "So, what did you usually do on your birthdays, then?" He asks as he leads me over to the living room. We sit close together on the couch, our legs touching.

"Sometimes my mom would invite Danielle to sleep over and we would do the typical hair braiding and making friendship bracelets thing. Once we drove out to Taco Terrace and I got a kids' meal. That was when they still had the indoor playground. For the most part, it was just another day. My mom really tried to make it special, though. We never had a lot of extra money, but every year she would put heart-shaped sticky notes on my door. One for every year of my age. Like when I was ten, there were ten hearts. She would write nice things about me on them."

"What did they say?"

"I wish I kept them. I don't really remember now. Probably things like she loved me, or she thought I had a good smile."

"You do." I can't help but smile at the compliment, which causes him to say "See?" and makes me roll my eyes.

"She always tried to have a gift for me to open, too. Usually, it was something from the clearance section at the grocery store, like bubbles she'd picked up for a few cents at the end of the summer season. But it was the hearts I really looked forward to. And her peach cake. She always made that for birthdays."

"That's right. I remember now. That cake was really good." He stretches out on the couch and lays his head on my lap. I absentmindedly run the fingers of my left hand through his hair while my other hand reaches over him to set my empty container on the coffee table.

"Yeah, it was. I have the recipe, but I've never tried to make it." My mom's peach cake was almost legendary. Friends would call to request it for special occasions.

"Do you want to try to bake it? I can help," Jake offers.

"Maybe one day, but right now, I want to stay just like this."

He only answers with a contented hum.

"Hey, Jake?"

"Yeah?' His eyes are still closed. My fingers go still as I gather my courage.

"What would you say if I suggested breaking our one rule?"

His brown eyes pop open and stare up at me. "I thought we did that when we decided to start dating?"

"True. But, technically, the rule was about not having sex, so we haven't actually broken it yet. What would you say if I wanted to?"

He sits up and faces me on the couch. I nod and bite the corner of my lip.

"I'd say hell yes! I'd break every rule in the world for you, Ace. Especially the stupid ones."

"That one was pretty stupid." I smile against his lips while he pulls me into a hungry kiss. I massage his tongue with mine for just a second before I pull back, leaving only an inch of space between us.

"Hey, Jake?" I say again.

He dips his head and hums a questioning noise into my collarbone as he palms my chest over the fabric of my dress.

"Do you think I could get a tour of your apartment? I haven't seen your bedroom."

His mouth finds mine again, and I let out a small squeal as he stands and lifts me. He wraps my legs around his waist, carrying me down the hall. When we reach the bed, he drops me onto the mattress, and I pull my dress over my head. I'm still turned on from our photo shoot, and I'm tired of denying how much I want him.

"Condom. Now."

"Always so bossy," he teases.

"Whatever. You love me."

We both freeze the second the words are out of my mouth. Then a slow smile spreads across his face, and he reaches under his mattress for a condom and strips himself out of his clothes.

He didn't deny it.

It's all I can think about until he has me seeing stars and my body is so relaxed that I can't think about anything at all.

Chapter 33

Alice

Jake is working so hard to fix up the studio. I know this has been his plan for a while, and once the space was available, I think he just needed to hear someone tell him it was a good idea. I'm not surprised to see how much he has accomplished since the last time I stopped by, but there's so much to take in, I'm not sure where to look first.

He tiled the wall behind the counter with thin bricks, and the grungy stained carpet has been removed. The exposed concrete floors have been stained and sealed, and now our business logo is painted directly in the middle. He designed it himself. The letter J is featured in bold print with a flowing cursive A overlapping slightly, and the words "Just Art" in an old-fashioned typeface underneath. The remaining walls are bright white, except for the mural that faces our front windows so it's visible from the street. Jake painted hands in all different sizes and colors holding paintbrushes, cameras, and books.

There are long, family-style tables and an eclectic collection of mismatched stools and chairs. Hazel is snoring on an overstuffed dog bed in the corner. He brings her to work every day. I bend down and give her one of the homemade peanut butter treats I've started keeping in a little tin in my purse for her. When I stand up, my eyes are drawn to the empty wooden bookshelf that stretches up to the ceiling. A sliding library ladder is attached.

Jake walks over and lays a hand on the middle shelf, at eye level. "We'll reserve this section for your stuff." He wants my books to have prime real estate.

I go to him and wrap my arms around his waist for a quick hug. After denying what I wanted for so long, it still feels weird to be able to touch him whenever I want.

"That sounds amazing. It's looking great in here."

He smiles down at me. "You like it?"

"Jake, I love it. Seriously. I can't believe how much you've accomplished by yourself. I'm sorry I couldn't be more help this week." I stretch my neck to look up at him.

He shakes his head, refusing to hear my apology. "You were where you needed to be."

I've been busy taking my dad to a few medical appointments. He's doing really well. Honestly, Earl Caulfield's like a new man. Or maybe more like the old version of him, the dad I remember from when my mom was still here. He's still going to therapy, and I've even started going to family sessions with him. I've also had a few individual sessions of my own to focus on my grief and anxiety. I can't believe I have Jake to thank for nudging us in that direction.

"I'm glad to finally have you back, though. I'm putting you to work today."

"Oh yeah, Boss?" I smile.

He groans and pulls me closer. "Good thing I'm not actually your boss, because we both know you'd never listen, and then I'd have to fire you. Which would be awkward with you owning half the studio."

"I'm not sure who taught you percentages, but five percent is way less than half."

He smirks. "Someone didn't read her contract carefully. We're in this fifty-fifty, Ace. Your letter is the same size as mine." He points to the logo on the floor, and I'm not sure how I didn't realize until now that the Just Art logo is made of our initials.

"Jake." I shake my head at him. There's no way the tiny nest egg I invested was enough to cover half of the ownership in a company. He just smiles down at me and raises his eyebrows, waiting for me to say more. "I didn't give you enough for that."

"See, that's where you're wrong. And we both know how much I love it when that happens." He chuckles and pulls me toward the chairs so we can sit and talk. "You've invested more time, energy, and support in me than anyone has in a long time. And, yes, you invested money, too. But you bring so much more to the table than your wallet, Alice. I couldn't have done this without you. This place belongs to you just as much as it belongs to me. We're in this together. You're stuck with me now."

"I can live with that," I say as I lean forward to kiss him. "Although, it might've been fun to say I was sleeping with the boss."

He hums into my mouth and says, "Is that your way of telling me we're trying a little role-play tonight?"

"You wish. But I do have a surprise for you. Guess what came today?" I break away to reach into my bag and pull out the album I ordered from Elliotte. "Our boudoir photos are finally here." I let out a little squeal when I hand it over to him.

His teeth skim over his bottom lip as he turns the pages. "This was the best idea I ever had."

I nod. "It really, really was. Look at this one." I point to the photo of him holding me on the bed. "That's my favorite."

Jake growls and sets the album down, then he launches into me for another kiss. My tongue has a mind of its own, and I'm practically levitating over him, pulling his face closer to mine, when we hear a throat clear.

"Hi, Mom." Jake takes the time to drop one last kiss on my forehead before he stands to greet Shelia. She hums a note of disapproval that makes me bristle, but I plaster on a smile and turn to face her. Jake and I weren't doing anything wrong by sitting here and sharing a kiss in the building we own, and I am not going to be shamed for being affectionate with her son. If anything, she should be able to understand why I fell for Jake.

"Hello." She nods curtly to both of us. "I came by to deliver this. It came to the house, and I thought it might be of interest." She hands Jake an envelope with his name on it that has clearly already been opened. There's a straight slit across the top because Shelia Gibson is the type of person who uses an actual letter opener.

Jake rolls his tongue over his teeth and pauses to take a deep breath. "Thanks." He takes the envelope from her and puts it in his back pocket without saying another word. He clearly wants her to go. Unfortunately, Shelia doesn't take the hint.

"Would you care to explain why an Explanation of Benefits for services provided by a mental health therapist was delivered to our house, Jacob? After all, you are still listed on our health insurance. Your father and I have a right to know what we are paying for." She waves a hand in my direction. "If you and this girl are already in need of professional counseling, I have my reservations about this business venture, and I have a responsibility as your mother to speak up."

Jake turns a chair to face her and sits back down, leaning back with his arms folded across his chest. "Do you really want to know, Mom? Because it sounds like you think you have it all figured out, and maybe you'd prefer to carry on believing your own version of events. Do you actually want me to tell you what I talk about in therapy *alone*?" He pins her with his stare.

I'm so proud of him for finally sticking up for himself, but this is uncomfortable to watch. At least, for once, I know this has nothing to do with me.

I feel like I'm intruding, so I start to take a step, but Jake's hand comes out to grab mine and keep me next to him. He wants me here.

He's calm as he tells his mom, "If you must know, most of my sessions are spent discussing what it's like to bend over backward for parents who don't return the same level of respect and refuse to acknowledge my effort. We talk about separating my own needs from your unrealistic expectations. We talk about what it was like to grow up in an environment short on affection but abundant with criticism. And we talk about what a pleasant relief it has been to find a partner who treats me like an equal and challenges me in new ways. Which is refreshing after spending a large chunk of my life being manipulated by the people who claimed to love me."

I squeeze Jake's hand. I know that was hard for him.

"Well. I see there was a misunderstanding about the letter, and you seem to be having difficulty managing the stress of this new…business." Again, Shelia waves one hand in the air, dismissing all the hard work Jake put into the remodel while she attempts to downplay her earlier accusations. "I'll come back when you've had a chance to get your emotions under control."

Jake scoffs. "Right. Sure. My emotions are the problem here. Did you hear a word I just said?"

"My ears work perfectly well, Jacob. To think I spent twenty-three years raising a young man who would stand here and call his own mother manipulative and uncaring."

Jake manages to keep a neutral expression on his face, but my heart cracks in half hearing his mother talk to him like this.

He stares back at Shelia. "I see. Once again, this is all about you. Look, Mom, if you don't want me on your insurance anymore, that's fine. I'll figure it out on my own. We've been looking into small business options anyway. But what we are not going to do is have you walking into our business and publicly questioning me about my medical records. You've chosen to cross a boundary. That's on you. Now I need you to leave." Jake's voice is icy and hard.

Shelia's eyes grow wide. I think she expected him to cave and apologize. Even I didn't expect him to kick her out. She's obviously not used to hearing him talk to her this way. Maybe he never has. If that's the case, it's been a long time coming.

I squeeze his hand again and try to show him with that small gesture that I'm right here and I'm proud of him.

"Shelia," I address her. Her eyes shift to me briefly, then she looks back to Jake. I know she thinks this is my fault somehow, like I'm stealing her baby boy right out from under her. She doesn't even want to look at me. Well, too bad. She can think whatever she wants. Jake and I are a team now. I know she has too much pride to leave just because Jake said so, but no good will come from having her try to stay right now, so I say, "I think Honey was looking for you. She was at The Blue Crab during the lunch rush. I bet you can still catch her."

Shelia nods once, then accepts my offer to save face and turns to go. Nothing is more important to Shelia Gibson than her pride. Even her own son, apparently. It's infuriating, but if we might be family one day we're going to have to find a way to understand each other. I can try to be the bigger person and model what that looks like.

Jake clings to my hand as we watch his mom walk away. Then he turns in his chair to lean his head against my shoulder. I rub my free hand up and down his back, trying to comfort him. He pulls me into his lap and holds me against his chest while he buries his face in my hair. He clutches me like he's drowning and I'm the life raft keeping him afloat. We sit quietly, and I let him hold me for as long as he needs. Hazel comes up and lays her head on his leg to let Jake know she's here for him, too.

I'm the first one to speak again. "That was intense."

He nods and sets me down gently so he can stand. He looks so drained. "I'm sorry, but I think I need to get out of here for a while. Come on, Hazel." He pats his leg, and she stretches and yawns before sauntering over to him.

"Don't apologize. Take some time. I'll stick around here for a while. Call me later?"

He nods once more and kisses my forehead, then Jake and Hazel leave, and I'm alone in the empty studio.

Chapter 34

Jake

I've been waiting for years to say those things to my mom. I thought when it finally happened I would feel proud or empowered, but instead the whole confrontation left me feeling like complete garbage. I don't think I did anything wrong, but I'm sure she would say the same thing on her end. She never thinks she's part of the problem, and I don't want to be like that. I'm willing to take ownership of my part in this weird dynamic with my parents, but I still don't understand what my part actually is.

I'm so exhausted I crash as soon as I'm home, even though it's barely lunchtime. Hazel comes to the bed and rests her face next to mine. She stays quiet, just letting me know she's here.

I pull out my phone and text Monica to ask if she happens to have any availability for a telehealth session today. Thankfully, she has a cancellation, so it isn't long before I'm logging on and talking to my therapist through my phone screen. We've been working together for a few months now, and it's getting much easier to vocalize the things I need to tell her, even if they are still embarrassing most of the time. I give her a brief overview of what happened today.

"Like I've told you before, my mom is…difficult. And sometimes I even worry it might be why I'm drawn to Alice. I don't know if that's healthy."

Logically, I know masculinity is a social construct or whatever, but I've never felt like less of a man than I do sitting here confessing my mommy issues and knowing I've been too much of a coward to confront them. Do I get off on fighting with Alice just because my mom gives me such a hard time about everything? That's pretty sick.

"Do you find it difficult to be around Alice?" Something about the way Monica words the question makes me pause before I answer. Sure, there are a lot of things about Alice that are hard to deal with. She's stubborn. She loves getting under my skin. She's pushy. She won't take no for an answer. She hates to admit when she's wrong, and her apologies still kind of suck. But she's really working on all of that stuff, and being around her? It's the easiest, most natural thing in the world. She's funny, and she's smart, and she pushes me to fight for what I want.

"No. Not at all. I like being with her. But we argue all the time."

"What do you argue about?"

"Mostly small things. We bicker over what show to watch or what to order for dinner. We can't agree on a paint color for the bathroom in the studio, and we have vastly different opinions about books." There are plenty of other examples. Like how she still freaks out if I try to buy her something as small as a soda. She's constantly misplacing important papers because she can't stick to a filing system. I could go on, but I'm not sure any of those things really matter. I'm starting to see where Monica's going with this. "When it comes to the big stuff, though, we're almost always on the same page. She loves the studio as much as I do. She goes out of her way to help me take care of Hazel. We have similar views about a lot of big-ticket items, like how neither of us wants to get married because we've both seen our parents get trapped in unhappy situations."

"It sounds like Alice is important to you. I can tell you've put a lot of thought into this."

"I think I love her," I admit.

"Have you told her that?"

I shake my head. "Not yet."

"Do you think you should?"

"I know I should, but I also know I need to talk to my parents about all of this. I can't keep asking Alice to ignore their prejudice against her or her family. It's not fair for me to put her in that position. Plus, I'm scared it will make her go back to hating me the way she used to." I scrub a hand down my face. "But it's not going to be an easy conversation. My parents aren't going to take it well. They're already upset with me."

"I've noticed you seem to focus a great deal on the opinions of others. Why do you think it matters so much to you if people think highly of you?"

My brow pulls tight, and I shake my head. "Everyone cares what people think."

"Do they?"

"Don't they? Doesn't everyone have a desire to be likable? I'm not sure I understand what you mean."

"What happens when you make a decision someone disagrees with?"

"They get mad."

"What else?"

"I feel guilty."

"Are you thinking about a specific example?"

"Maybe when I got my tattoos? My parents were disappointed. They hate them. This is going to be so much worse. They've explicitly said they don't want me to be with Alice."

"And it bothers you when they are disappointed?"

"I wish it didn't. But yeah. My mom said some stuff today that really hurt. I've spent so much time trying to make her and my dad proud. Like maybe if I could do everything right, they could focus on how happy I make them rather than how miserable they make themselves. As if I could fix it by receiving another perfect report card or winning another game. It's hard to accept it's not going to happen. Nothing will ever be good enough, no matter what I do."

"After their initial disappointment, what was the effect of your decision to get a tattoo? Did anyone actually suffer because of it? Do you believe you would make the same choice again, given the option?"

I nod. I would, and I did. I got my second sleeve done, even though I knew it would piss them off. "I guess nothing really happened. I have to deal with a few sighs and passive-aggressive comments from my mom now. She asks me to wear long sleeves to holiday parties, but that's about it. My dad just pretends he can't see them. It's annoying, but it's not like I expected them to open a social media account to show off my ink. The world kept spinning."

"Body modifications like piercings and tattoos are morally neutral, just like the clothes we wear or the hairstyles we choose. Other people might carry their own feelings about them, but those feelings are theirs to hold. You are not responsible for other people's reactions or emotions when it comes to the morally neutral choices you make for your own life."

I have to clear my throat because that last sentence hit me like a sucker punch. She's right. None of the things my parents are upset with me about are life-or-death decisions. Does it really matter in the end if they don't like my career choice, or the fact that I'm going to therapy, or Alice's family not having as much money as they do? If it's true there are no serious consequences for any of the things causing me so much stress, then why am I still so nervous about disappointing my mom and dad?

"I think it's more that I know the choices I'm making are going to lead to a lot of rejection." Choosing Alice will probably destroy any shot at rebuilding a relationship with my parents, and yet I'm doing it on purpose. Even though I know they're wrong, the weight of this kind of choice is still a lot.

"It's true, that can happen sometimes. Although, we never truly know how others will respond until we are in the situation, and regardless of how they handle their emotions or behaviors, we are still only responsible for our own feelings and actions. Still, it's hard when we believe that a lack of perfection will equal rejection." Monica's timer beeps off-screen. "That's our time, Jake. But before we go, I want to remind you that you don't have to be perfect to be loved. But we do need to love ourselves first, and part of loving ourselves means knowing we deserve to be treated with respect."

I thank her and hang up. I know what I need to do, but I'm not looking forward to it.

When I pull up to the house, Ms. Honey waves to me from the rocking chair on her front porch across the street. I nod at her, then I knock before letting myself in through my parents' unlocked front door. They're in the middle of an argument and I hear my name, which is no surprise. What I came here to say won't make it any better. But no matter how much I wish things were different, I can't change them any more than they can change me. Like Monica said, all I can do is focus on myself and the way I want to act toward the people who matter to me. Right now, that means protecting Alice and myself from this toxicity.

I clear my throat. Both of them stop mid-sentence and turn in my direction. They were so busy arguing they didn't notice me come in.

"Hi. I want to talk about what happened at the studio."

"Ah yes, the studio. The waterlogged building where our son is offering his coloring book classes. What's happened now? What is he talking about?" My dad asks my mother, as if I can't speak for myself. I pull my shoulders back and force myself to take a long breath through my nose and let it out slowly. I won't let them get to me. Not this time.

"There was a misunderstanding earlier. It's been handled," my mom tries to assure him.

I cut her off. "No one misunderstood anything. Your intentions were clear, and Alice deserves a lot more respect from both of you. Quite frankly, so do I. But I've accepted that's not likely to happen in this lifetime, so I only ask that you don't treat her like that again."

"Don't be ridiculous. It's not as though this little fling with that girl will go anywhere." My mom tilts her head up. It's her version of rolling her eyes, which she won't do because it's bad manners, although apparently disparaging my girlfriend in front of me is within the etiquette guidelines. I'm so over this.

"Do not speak about her that way. Alice has a name, and if you'd like to remain on civil terms with me, you need to learn to use it."

She gasps and grabs the neckline of her sweater. "Do you see what this girl is doing to you? I cannot believe the way you are speaking to me today. Your own mother. Shameful is what it is."

My dad glares at me and lets out a low groan of disapproval.

I'm done.

"You know what? You're right, Mom. It is a shame. It's a shame I've let this go on as long as it has. Look, Alice is important to me. She has always been important to me, and I'm not going to allow anyone to treat her this way. Even you. Especially you."

"What are you saying, Jacob?"

Isn't it obvious?

"I will not lose Alice. I'd rather not lose you either, but if you make me choose, you will not like the outcome."

Mom is taken aback for a second, then she straightens her shoulders. "I see."

We're frozen in a silent stand-off, and I can hear the antique clock on the mantle ticking the seconds away. I will maintain this uncomfortable eye contact for as long as it takes.

Finally, Mom speaks again. "Honey Daniels was right."

"What are you talking about?" What would Ms. Honey have to say about this?

"She saw this coming, and she told me as much at the wedding. She thought you and *Alice* looked smitten while you were dancing. It was her opinion I was being too harsh on you both. I thought it was quite an overstep, but clearly you share her view. I will not apologize for wanting the best for my son. Regardless, we can certainly be civil, can't we Ward?"

"What kind of question is that? We've always been civil with the girl."

"Alice," I growl. "Use. Her. Name."

"Yes, Alice," my father agrees. "Fine. Are we done with this little display?"

It's not the complete turn-around I was hoping for, but it's as good as I'm going to get tonight, and probably more than I expected. I know most of their frustration has nothing to do with Alice. It's me. They think I'm a disappointment and maybe, according to their definition, I am.

I take a step forward.

I did drop out of school. I did cover my body in ink. I did choose an unstable career path. And yes, I did fall for a girl from the other side of town. Those were all things I needed to do to find myself and be happy, and despite what my parents think, they are all morally neutral. I haven't done anything wrong. Just because someone drew a map for my life doesn't mean I have to follow the path they laid out. If they're upset or disappointed, those are *their* feelings to hold.

"I love you, both." I hold out my arms and offer my mom a hug, which she awkwardly accepts. She leans into me sideways and pats my arm before she pulls away. Never much for affection, my dad only clears his throat and nods.

Then I let go.

I don't know if they realize they get to decide if this is a goodbye. Maybe they'll come around one day, and I hope they do. But their choices are on them. My future is waiting outside of this house.

Chapter 35

Alice

I yawn and force myself to wake up. It's August twenty-eighth, but the one person I want to celebrate with is no longer here. My birthday is the day I miss my mom the most.

It takes me a hot minute to drag myself away from the warmth of my bed. When I open the door, my eyes need a few seconds to adjust to what I'm seeing. There's a balloon tied to my chair and a single cupcake with blue icing sits at my place at the table. The walls are covered with heart-shaped sticky notes. There must be hundreds of them.

I turn to see Jake standing next to my dad in the living room.

"Happy birthday, Alice." Dad nods at me. His beard is trimmed, and I think he actually ironed his shirt.

Jake's wearing a small, bashful smile, waiting for me to take it all in. There are so many little hearts in every color imaginable. Each one has something written on it, and in the center of them all is a banner that says "Things We Love About Alice."

They did this for me? I blink and walk slowly to the wall and start to read.

Your smile.

Your pranks.

The way you push me to be better.

I recognize Jake's handwriting as I take a few hearts down to hold. The ones from him have hand-drawn cartoons next to the words.

I also recognize Danielle's *Your amazing advice.* And *My beautiful, resilient bestie.* I finally told her about Owen the other day, and we had a tearful look through the boudoir photos while I told her how Jake's idea helped me heal.

Even Honey has a note on the wall that says *My favorite book club partner.*

My dad added some of his own, too. I notice his shaky chicken scratch.

You're a good daughter.

Thank you for making my lunches.

But what shocks me the most are the ones I haven't seen for years. I gulp in a sob and my eyes are immediately filled with tears that make it hard to read my mom's handwriting.

"You found them?"

Jake nods and takes a step closer, but he still gives me enough space to have this moment for myself. "Your mom kept all of them. Earl had the box in the attic."

"Guess there are a few perks to never throwing anything away." Dad shrugs, but his voice is gruff with the emotion he's clearly trying to contain.

I run my fingers along the edge of each pink and purple heart as I stare in disbelief at my mother's words.

You can read!

Such a big helper for Mommy.

I love your knock-knock jokes. So funny!

I can't believe you have your driver's license.

They're all here. Every one of my mom's notes from nineteen years of birthdays. The sticky backs have long since lost their tack, so they're attached to the wall with little dots of poster putty. Somehow, I know Jake didn't want to risk using tape and ripping them. Such a tiny, thoughtful gesture brings even more sobs. I had no idea my parents kept all of these. My face is wet with tears and snot while I full-on ugly cry.

"Dad, this is amazing."

My dad walks over and wraps his arms around me. The hug is stiff. It's the first one we've exchanged in a long time, but he's trying. He's working so hard to get better. I squeeze back tightly before he pulls away to make space for the other man in my life.

"Jake." My voice breaks as he comes up next to me.

He cups my cheeks with both hands and uses his thumbs to brush some of my tears away. I must look like such a mess. I'm still in my pajama pants and Jake's old tee. I haven't even brushed my hair or my teeth, and now there is a river of liquid flowing down my face.

"Happy birthday, Alice." He pulls me against him for another hug before he says, "There's one more thing." He puts a small green paper heart in my hand. I look down and read the words in his handwriting. *You were right. I do love you.*

I blink up at him. My heart is so full that I'm vaguely worried I might explode. "Do you have a pen?" I manage to rasp.

He quirks an eyebrow, amused, and reaches down to grab one from the coffee table. I lean against his chest and write my own message underneath his words. *I love you, too.* I press the heart back into his hand. He laughs when he sees I also circled the part where he admitted I was right, and I added another word above that sentence: *Duh.*

Epilogue

Two Years Later

Alice

"**A**re you sure you're ready for this?"

"Not my first time under the gun, Ace." Jake winks and turns around to face me while he walks backward through the drizzling rain. He holds up both arms, showcasing his artwork. "Are you sure *you're* ready? No chickening out now. We're here."

"I'm good. Not my first time either," I remind him, pointing at my neck.

Despite his teasing, I know if I really did change my mind about this one, he wouldn't hold it against me. But it doesn't matter, I'm not backing down. I've never been more ready for anything.

He pulls the door open and waits while I walk inside ahead of him. We both shake the rain from our hair, and I shiver when a blast of air conditioning meets my wet skin.

"Welcome to Ink. I'm the artist on staff today. Do you have an appointment?" The woman at the counter asks.

"Sure do."

We're here on the two-year anniversary of the storm that threw us together so we can get the matching funnel cloud tattoos Jake designed. After surviving a literal hurricane and tornado and getting swept up in our own stormy romance, it seemed fitting. We have a lot to celebrate.

Just Art is doing so well we've opened a second location in Marnock this year. Shelia even stopped by the opening to say hello.

Things are still strained with Jake's parents, and he has decided to keep contact limited. He doesn't want to cut them off completely since it is almost impossible not to cross paths in a town as small as ours, and he still has hope they can repair the damage that's been done. But he's no longer the one to initiate interactions with them. If they want to have a relationship with their son, they need to come to him. At least for now, things between us and his family are peaceful when we are in the same space.

I created an indie imprint to help other authors publish their work, and I signed a contract last week with my first writer. My own books don't bring in a ton of income, but they have steady sales, and Jake draws all the artwork for them. I even got a five-star review recently from someone with the username Ratty Professor that said *I may have previously misjudged this author. She has shown a lot of growth in her recent work.* That one definitely made me smile.

Jake pulls a folded piece of paper out of his pocket and shows the tattoo artist the sketch he drew. It's small and tasteful, just a few squiggly lines. The swirl almost looks like someone was testing to see if a pen ran out of ink, except when you look closely it's much more intentional. There's an almost floral flourish to it. I'm so excited to have a tiny piece of Jake's art with me, permanently.

"Nice. Where would you like to place these?"

Jake points to his chest. He plans to put his next to the tattoo he surprised me with last month. He got an Ace of Hearts card done right over his heart.

"And you?" The receptionist turns to me.

I swallow and gather my nerves. I haven't talked to Jake about this idea yet, but I know where I want mine.

"Um, I was thinking right here." I point to my left ring finger.

Jake looks at me. "Does that mean what I think it means?"

I nod, smiling cautiously. I'm not sure how he feels about this. I still don't want to get married in the traditional sense. But I do want the promise of forever with him.

"You about to get down on one knee for me, Alice?" His grin is contagious.

"Nah. I'm not doing this with your crotch in my face."

"I mean, it wouldn't hurt your chances," he teases.

"Are you going to let me do this or not?"

"By all means." He makes a sweeping gesture to signify that I have the floor.

I take a breath and look up into his eyes. "Jacob Gibson, against all odds I seem to have fallen completely and totally in love with you. Marriage is still off the table, but will you commit to infinity with me and be my partner through whatever additional crazy storms life throws at us? Turns out you're pretty great at that, and I really want to keep you around."

"Hell yes, I'm going to be yours to annoy and cherish forever." He picks me up and sets me on the checkout desk so he can kiss me the way he wants to: deeply, with a lot of tongue. The artist clears her throat, but Jake holds up one finger for her to please give us a minute. He breaks the kiss but keeps his forehead connected to mine as he reaches into his jacket pocket to pull out a little velvet box. "You beat me to it, but we are definitely on the same page. I had a whole plan. I was going to take you to dinner in Marnock after this, then drive out to Uncle Tim's cottage and give this to you there. I booked it for the weekend. There are real sheets on the bed now and everything."

I laugh while he lifts the lid from the box to reveal a silver locket. The front is engraved with our initials in the same style as the Just Art logo. When I open the heart-shaped pendant, instead of a photo, there is a tiny hand-drawn portrait of the two of us with Hazel in the middle. I miss her so much.

Tears spring to my eyes while he hooks the necklace around me. It figures, he already had a plan. "Tell me more about this grand gesture at the cottage. What would you have said?"

He doesn't even take a second to think before he recites, "Alice Caulfield, you're the most important person in my life, and I never want to spend another day without you. I'm sorry we wasted so much time fighting this, and I'm so glad that storm finally pushed us together. Please commit to making me the happiest man on the planet by agreeing to never marry me."

"I think that can be arranged."

"Perfect. Then by the power of this tattoo parlor, in front of absolutely no one except...sorry what was your name?" he asks our artist.

"Molly." She pops her gum. Molly seems mildly amused by us, but mostly bored.

"Then with Molly as our witness, do you hereby swear to commit to spend forever with me?" Jake asks.

"I do."

"Cool. I do, too."

My arms still hang loosely around his neck, and I wrap my feet around his waist to pull him in for one more kiss before he spins us and carries me over to the chair. I hear the low buzz of the needle, and I register when it pricks my skin, but I barely feel a thing because I'm too busy floating on a cloud of my own joy.

We're here, sticking it out with each other every day, because it's the choice we wake up and make over and over again. I choose him, and he chooses me. We don't need the ceremony or fanfare. We don't want all the drama that comes with big weddings. Ironic, maybe, considering how this all started. But all Jake and I need is each other.

He decides to get his funnel cloud on his finger as well, and it doesn't take long before the tiny tattoos are finished. Jake pays Molly, making sure to leave a large tip to make up for shushing her earlier.

Then he reaches out for me, and I walk out into the world for the first time with my new ink, hand-in-hand with the last person on Earth I ever expected to call mine.

The rain is coming down harder now. We ignore it as Jake pulls me to his body. He bends toward me, and as the water soaks into our clothes, I stand on my tiptoes, stretching up to meet his lips. Nothing else in my life has ever felt as right as it does to be standing here in the rain with Jacob Freaking Gibson.

"You're stuck with me now, Ace. It's in writing." He holds up his left hand, then he takes mine and brings my ring finger to his lips, careful to keep his touch near my knuckles and away from the newly sensitive skin.

I grab his jacket and pull him back for one more kiss. "You won't hear any arguments from me."

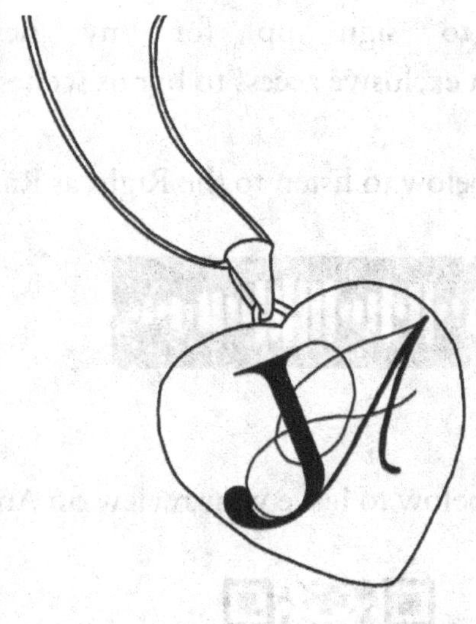

Thank you for reading!

If you enjoyed this book, please be sure to leave a review on platforms like Amazon or Goodreads and share your thoughts on social media. Your reviews help independent authors so much! Your support means the world to me.

Don't forget to sign up for my newsletter at stephaniegiese.com to get exclusive access to bonus scenes!

Scan the Spotify code below to listen to the Right as Rain playlist.

Scan the QR code below to leave your review on Amazon.

What's Next in North Bay?

What did Shelley's text messages to Jordan say? Find Out in **Way Off Base**, Book 3 in the North Bay Series. Turn the page for a sneak peek!

An Excerpt from

Way Off Base

Shelley

I scream in frustration and pull a pillow over my face to muffle the noise. I can't do it. No matter what I try, just like every other time, nothing happens. It's been almost forty minutes, and I give up. My body is broken, and it doesn't matter how many times or how many different ways I attempt, I'm never going to be able to get there. The Petal Pulverizer toy lying next to me is just the latest in a long line of failed gadgets. Why is it so easy for everyone else? The last two guys I dated told me it was impossible for them to please a woman who doesn't know her own body well enough to know what she wants. I take the toy and throw it at the wall, but because I can't do anything right today, it falls short and lands softly on the carpet.

When I spoke to my doctor at my annual exam, she told me I'm probably just too in my head about it and to try to relax. Easier said than done. Then she recommended seeking out a sex therapist. Which I did, and that doctor suggested toys and frequent solo sessions to learn my body. The sex therapist also told me to "stop trying so hard to reach the destination and learn to enjoy the journey." As if I can just turn off my entire personality. I try hard. It's who I am. Normally my efforts produce results, like getting into law school at Franklin Monroe. But all my trying means nothing when it comes to getting my body to cooperate.

Could this be any more humiliating?

I pick up my phone and shoot off a text to the group chat with my sisters. Madison answers immediately because she's the one who recommended the Petal Pulverizer.

Me: *That one was also a no-go.*

Mads: *Dang. I was really pulling for that one. Get it?*

Me: *Ew. Shut up. I hate you.*

I sigh. My siblings love stupid puns, but I don't have the patience for any more jokes about this. Especially bad ones. When our youngest sister, Mandy, finally chimes in at least she seems to sense my need for them to take me seriously.

Mandy: *Nah. You love us. But I'm running out of ideas. Maybe try to get in touch with Josephine Wilson? Isn't this sort of what she does now?*

Me: *That's actually not a bad idea.*

Mandy replies with a gif of a cartoon mouse taking a bow and the words "you're welcome" in huge capital letters underneath.

Jo and I were on the track team together back in Idaho. We were never super close, but we've always been friendly in the superficial way where we like each other's posts online, and we say hi if one of us notices the other out in public when I'm home visiting. Mandy's right, this is kind of what Jo does now. I've seen her talking about her research on social media. She's working on her master's thesis, researching the correlation between unpaid female domestic labor and the orgasm gap. I remember one of the headlines she shared recently was *Primary Parents Don't Put Out: Equal Partnerships Achieve Higher Success Rates, Both In and Out of the Bedroom.* As a single first-year law student, I don't really fit her core demographic, but if anyone we know might have a valid, scientific opinion about what's going on with me, it will be Josephine Wilson.

Right. I can do this.

Before I chicken out, I create a new memo in my voice recording app explaining what's going on with me and asking for her advice.

Hey, Jo. It's Shelley Miller. I know it's been a while since we've talked, but I'm following your work and cheering you on from the sidelines. I wondered if you might have some advice? Remember that article you posted a few weeks ago that said up to fifteen percent of women have never, um, achieved a climax? Uh, well, I think, or I should say I know I'm in that camp, unfortunately. And I'm just wondering if you have any, like, professional advice for people in my…situation? I've already been to two doctors. I don't know what's wrong with me or my body, and I would love to finally get an answer. Do you think we might be able to chat when you have a free minute? Sorry, I know this is awkward. Thanks for considering."

I take a breath and gather my courage, then type "Jo" into the search area. It brings up my J contacts, and I click her name quickly to send the message, then I slam my phone face down on the bed. *Just breathe.* Nothing wrong with seeking an opinion from a professional.

It's not long before the phone buzzes.

I swallow and take another calming breath, trying to be mature about this whole thing. The plan to act like an adult immediately goes out the window when I see the text is from my brother's roommate.

Jordan: *Hey, Shelley. I think you intended this for someone else.*

My stomach drops straight through my feet.

No. No no no no no. This cannot be happening.

I sent Jordan that message?

Jordan. As in my professional baseball-playing brother's best friend and teammate. The guy Mike currently lives with, and the one on whom I've been crushing since the first time we met last year. That Jordan? The one with the great smile who makes the most intense eye contact I've ever experienced. *That's* the one whose name I must have accidentally clicked because it's listed alphabetically right before Josephine in my contacts? Jordan just heard me say out loud, in my own voice, that I can't climax.

Awesome.

Me: *Sorry. I can't respond to you right now because my soul left my body and I have expired.*

Jordan: *OK. R.I.P. But it's sad knowing you're gone before you ever really lived.*

Me: *OMG. Stop. Can we please pretend this never happened?*

Jordan: *Sure. If that's what you want. But before I let it go...*

Acknowledgements

It takes so many people to make a book happen! First, thank you to my family for your patience and support. To my husband, Eddie, and our children: Nick, Abigail, Donny, Ana, and Penelope, I appreciate the sacrifices you make so I have the time and space to do the work that feeds my soul. To my mom, Teri Wilkins, thanks for answering all my late-night grammar questions. There will always be errant commas, but at least now I (mostly) understand the conditional tense.

To my daughter, Abigail, your beautiful, vibrant illustrations add so much life to these pages.

My cover designer, Rachel Adams-Howard, as always, I am in love with your work. I bow down to your ability to translate my vague descriptions into something real.

To my editor, Denise Drapeau, for the extra time and effort you poured into Jake and Alice's story. This was a tough one, but we did it!

To my ARC and street team, I quite literally could not do this job without you and your amazing encouragement and support. I love every one of you more than you will ever know.

And a special thanks to the readers, especially those in the BookTok community. You've built something magical, and I'm honored to have played a small part in it.

About the Author

Stephanie Giese lives in Florida with her large family and a very naughty beagle. She writes stories with humor and heart that have a strong focus on mental health, treatment, and consent.

www.ingramcontent.com/pod-product-compliance
Lightning Source LLC
Chambersburg PA
CBHW011035190726
48290CB00011B/2853